8.45

Voices of a Place

LIBRARY ST. MARY'S COLLEGE

Robert Dawson
From the Great Central Valley Project

818.54
H274

Voices of a Place

*Social and Literary Essays
from the Other California*

Gerald Haslam

WITHDRAWI

172414
DMB
Devil Mountain Books
P.O. Box 4115
Walnut Creek, California 94596

LIBRARY ST. MARY'S COLLEGE

Acknowledgment is made to the editors of the *Nation*, the *Californians, Bakersfield Lifestyle, Western American Literature, Pacific Discovery,* and *California English*, where some of the essays in this collection originally appeared.

Gerald Haslam

Voices of a Place

*Social and Literary Essays
from the Other California*

© *1987 by Gerald Haslam*

**DEVIL MOUNTAIN BOOKS, P.O. BOX 4115,
WALNUT CREEK, CA 94596. ALL RIGHTS RESERVED.**

No part of this work may be reproduced or used in any form or by any means—graphic, electronic, or mechanical, including photocopying, recording, taping, or information and retrieval systems—without written permission from the publisher. Manufactured in the United States of America.

Design and Cover / Wayne Gallup
Type / Encore Typesetting, Concord, CA
Typestyle: Century

**LIBRARY OF CONGRESS CATALOG CARD NUMBER: 87-70566
ISBN: 0-915685-05-1**

7890•54321

For William W. Haslam, my Uncle Willie,
and
Charlotte M. Epp, my Aunt Marge,
always willing to listen, always ready to debate.

CONTENTS

Foreword

In discussing Gerry Haslam's short stories, critics—myself included—invariably dwell on their regionalism, their Westernness, their assured place in the literature of California. All that is true, and yet I ask myself why a city boy from the East like me is such a fan of Haslam's work. I think I may have spent a night in a motel in Bakersfield once . . . or was it Fresno or Modesto? I know I've pulled off the I-5 at an A&W for root beer floats. I've certainly driven through the Great Central Valley many times on my way to or from Sequoia, Yosemite, the Bay Area, or the Gold Rush country, and I've always been somewhat in awe of my realization that most of our nation gets all of its grapes and olives and almonds from the outlying fields. I've had students who came from the valley to study nearer the beach, and a lot of them actually returned to the valley. I've been there in July when you'd swear the air-conditioning wasn't even turned on. But I've never really *been* there—I haven't had a single beer at the Tejon Club.

So why do I hold Haslam among those writers of short fiction such as Carver, Bukowski, Barthelme, and Fante that I most enjoy sitting down to read? Partly no doubt because I've always wondered as I rode through the valley what it *would* be like to live there. Partly because the valley has become, like Paris, a fact of the literary and mythic consciousness even of those who have never been within a thousand miles of it. Partly because there are bars in Seal Beach and Signal Hill, California, in Tulsa and Tucson that could be or should be in Oildale— working class bars near onshore or offshore rigs or in any neighborhood where men still work hard enough to come home with a ring of grime around their blue collars.

But mostly I love Haslam's stuff for the humor and tribulations and triumphs that impart to his work the potential universal appeal of a Faulkner, a Turgenev, or a Twain, and for the genius of dialectal realism, the large-souled sympathies, and the moral integrity of the author.

These qualities are not lacking in the essays collected here. I did not by any means enjoy them less than his stories; in fact *I learned even more from them* because so much fascinating information has to be left on the cutting room floor of that most single-minded of tasks, the short story. The essays give us the *why* of the way Haslam's characters think and act.

Ask any farmer in Iowa whether economics has relevance to his life. These essays explore the natural and economic and demographic history of the valley, and they are all the more timely with the area possibly standing on the brink of another depression. Anyone possessed of a natural curiosity should find himself absorbed in this portrait of a place where the people are not yet computerized. He may even find himself learning to speak the language, just like myownself.

Gerald Locklin
California State University
at Long Beach

Preface

In a letter dated September 26, 1975, Carey McWilliams paid me perhaps the highest compliment I've ever received as a writer. I had proposed an article for the *Nation* on the Posse Commitatus, and Carey responded, "It is a good subject particularly if looked at in your style and manner, that is, not hysterically, but with coolness and curiosity."

I hope these essays display coolness and curiosity along with concern and competence. They have been selected not as a sampler of all the subjects I've explored and styles I've employed over the past twenty years, but in the hope that they give genuine sense of the golden state's complexity by exploring some people, some places, some activities that do not conform to this state's stereotype. Since I am rooted in what has been called "the other California," no other locale of the land or the heart more intrigues me. It is, to borrow Judith Wright's eloquence, "my blood's country."

The essays collected in this volume were written for the *Nation*, the *Californians, Bakersfield Lifestyle, Western American Literature, Pacific Discovery,* and *California English.* Over the years other essays of mine have appeared in journals as various as *Voices: The Art and Science of Psychotherapy* and *California Magazine, Poets & Writers* and *Etc.: A Review of General Semantics*—nearly a hundred different periodicals. Each essay was a unique experience, a unique challenge.

"You can't write writing," Wendell Johnson once noted, and he was absolutely correct. It is an enduring pleasure to work my way through a complex of ideas and commit them to paper but, in retrospect, the assignments done for Carey at the *Nation* were especially satisfying. He was one of many fine editors with whom I have been lucky enough to work: Tom Lyon, Daryln Brewer, S.I. Hayakawa, Dan Warrick, Art Seidenbaum, Tom Liggett, Art Cuelho, et al.

It's been a long passage from bonehead English at Bakersfield Junior College in 1955, and a number of dedicated teachers and friends have helped: Dorothy Overly, Brother Leonard, Eddie Lopez, Sam Bullen, Larry Press, Charles Blackburn, Gerry Locklin, Jim Maguire, Bob Dantzler, Clark and Barbara Sturges and, of course, my folks, Speck and Lorraine Haslam—the list could be long indeed. Most important has been my wife, Jan, who married me when I was an oilfield roughneck and had slim prospects, and who has seen me through college and career. The point is that it has taken considerable help and that I've enjoyed the journey.

VOICES OF A PLACE   [1986]

Dawn after a rain in the Great Central Valley of California: to the east, a veneer of orange rims the crest of the Sierra Nevada, a thin electric line against nearly starless indigo, then the sky becomes a cantaloupe slice and sounds rise: a chorale of birds; far in the distance, roosters are interrupted by the cough and bawl of a reluctant tractor; at a diner, laughter accompanies first cups of watery coffee. Finally, the sun pops free from the Sierra's ragged crest and it is time, it is time . . .

Everything smelled good when you got up, and it was cool. I used to like the way the things smelled in the morning most of all.

        Peter Epp, Jr., farmer, 1952

If I were to live again, I would want to come to manhood in the lee of Lassen and Shasta. There it seems to me is the cor cordium *of California.*

        Lawrence Clark Powell, writer, 1978

They drove through Tehachapi in the morning glow, and the sun came up behind them, and then suddenly they saw the great valley below them. Al jammed on the brake and stopped in the middle of the road, and, "Jesus Christ! Look!" he said. The vineyards, the orchards, the great flat valley, green and beautiful, the trees set in rows, and the farm houses.

        John Steinbeck, writer, 1939

    This vast cleft in the middle of California is one of the world's largest valleys—over 400 miles long and 50 miles wide. Geologically, it is a trough between the Coast Ranges and the

Sierra Nevada, with the Cascades bordering it above and the Tehachapis marking it below. The only significant break in its generally flat topography is an intrusion of plio-pleistocene volcanic rock in its upper reaches, the Sutter Buttes. It drains two great river systems—the Sacramento flowing from the north, the San Joaquin from the south—which have created paired vales within this vast valley. They constitute the world's richest agricultural region, rice and alfalfa more commonly grown north of the state capital in Sacramento, grapes and cotton typifying the larger and more intensely developed south.

Socially and economically as well as geographically, the valley can—perhaps should—be divided into three subregions: the Sacramento and the San Joaquin Valleys separated by the Sac-Joaquin Delta, an elongated riverine ganglia of streams, marshes and islands extending roughly from Stockton to the west, connecting interior California with the Bay Area and the sea. In any case, the Great Central Valley—whatever its subregions—defies the state's flashy stereotype: it is a land in which raw, physical labor has attracted people of all colors willing to work those unforgiving fields. Scuffed boots, not Gucci loafers, characterize it.

Today, when natives return, they find cultivated fields where a year ago they hunted rabbits, stucco houses where ten years before almonds were harvested, McDonald's homogeneity replacing the Chat'n'Chew Cafe's intimacy. Amidst the area's considerable wealth, they discover the stumps of antique groves cut and torn from the earth, favorite streams dammed and tamed, old stores boarded and blank, and they die a little.

I still love Chico but . . . I don't know . . . it seems so big *anymore.*

Marie Johnson, housewife, 1984

I saw changes all around me and some were good,
but I hardly recognized my side of town.

2

They tore down the swinging casing from the cottonwood,
and that tree was all that marked familiar ground.

Merle Haggard, balladeer, 1974

Even before there were humans to observe it, the valley was changing. For millions of years it was a shallow sea. After mountains uplifted, "there were extensive lakes formed by flood-season overflow in both the Sacramento and San Joaquin Valleys," reports geologist Gordon B. Oakeshott. A hundred years ago, William Henry Brewer called part of it "a plain of absolute desolation." Despite stretches of what could fairly be described as desert, especially on its west side, it was veined by Sierran rivers and blocked by marshes. During this century, those rivers have been dammed and their waters redirected; most of the marshes are gone.

American settlement has accelerated and directed change, and that settlement has itself been a response to the world's and nation's population explosion: agricultural technology leading to greater and more efficient use of land, so that the valley's apparently inexhaustible larder makes population growth possible which, in turn, creates the demand for more produce. The affluence produced by that cycle then attracts urban dwellers, leading to the paving of farmland as well as both the agricultural conversion of the little remaining virgin soil and chemically intense cultivation of existing farms, what has been described as land being used to convert petroleum into produce.

What the latter leads to is still in question, although evidence of accumulating chemical toxins is becoming undeniable: "In the entire San Joaquin Valley," writes Jane Kay, "more than one quarter of the usable ground water, or thirty million acre feet, is polluted with DBCP." Agricultural runoff, she points out, is now one of the state's major pollution sources. Norman Crow, a prominent grower in Stanislaus County, counters by claiming, "As farmers, we're probably the greatest environmentalists. We see every part of every tree, every acre of land. I'd love it if I didn't have to use these chemicals."

LIBRARY ST. MARY'S COLLEGE

Unfortunately, he does have to use them, and evidence of contamination continues mounting.

It is also important to note that the valley not only boasts greater agricultural riches than most nations, but also richer petroleum resources than all but a handful; one county, Kern, which has been called the cradle of California's oil industry, produces considerably more of that commodity than some OPEC nations. This is also a source of both riches and anguish, the industry indicted for various forms of pollution, for economic instability in the face of international competition, and for a history of less-than-enlightened social practices, while at the same time it offers both vital energy resources and an abundance of jobs during good times.

I come here from Texas because there was work, and I been after it ever since. You pull them slips, you dump that mud, and the boss pays you. That's what it's all about.

"Brownie" Brown, driller, 1961

Oil production in Kern County is a technological miracle. Oil around here is heavy, almost like tar, and normal production methods can't pull it out of the ground efficiently. In the Sixties, however, scientists came up with an "enhanced" recovery process that injects steam into the deposits to get the oil flowing.

Roger Neal, writer, 1985

How important is this region to the state? Let Irving Stone answer: "Without this central valley, this modern-day Valley of the Nile, California would be a magnificent front, able to support less than half its population, hollow at its economic core."

Still, change is what natives notice, and people are the problem: their technology, their complexity and, most profoundly, their numbers. This greatest agricultural region on earth may stand as a paradigm for the planet . . .

Except for the lupins and poppies, which covered the valley in the spring, the country was semi-desert and the climate was horrible, with pea-soup fog in the winter, and 110 degrees in the summer. No one ever thought that the valley would be covered with orchards and vineyards as it is today.

Arnold "Jefe" Rojas, vaquero, 1985

No natural landscapes of California have been so altered by man as its bottomlands. The grass-rich stretches of the Great Central Valley are, for the most part, lost to orchards and vineyards, cotton and alfalfa fields. Many miles of curving green ribbon along its water courses have been eradicated, replaced by the sterile concrete of flood control and navigation channels. Most of the tule marshes of the Delta country are now neatly diked rice paddies.

Elna Bakker, ecologist, 1971

It used to be when I was coming off the Grapevine looking out over the southern San Joaquin Valley on a clear night, I could see only scattered lights—the column of white in one lane, red in another—of cars on Highway 99; a glow from Bakersfield thirty miles off in the distance; and only a few lights in the Wheeler Ridge oil field to the left and the Tejon Ranch farmlands to the right. Now there are lights everywhere.

William Rintoul, journalist, 1985

Originally three natural communities characterized the Great Central Valley: riverlands, with dense riparian forests; marshes and shallow lakes; vast prairies covered principally with perennial bunchgrasses. All have been dramatically altered—maimed, some say. Early travelers found the valley a difficult yet rich environment: to the south, for example, four streams, the Kern, Tule, Kaweah and Kings Rivers, fed two massive, shallow, almost-unnavigable lakes that were surrounded by vegetation and filled with waterfowl. Travelers

5

found the dry prairies blocked by icy rivers with often rampant riverine forests extending parallel to their banks as far as the land retained moisture, sometimes hundreds of yards. But most memorable to those passing through the valley were the prairies themselves.

Evidence of the area's scant rainfall surrounded travelers on the grassland; despite its marshes and rivers, this was essentially a land of low precipitation, with five-to-twenty inches a year falling, nearly all during the winter, and was periodically drought-stricken.

The Central Valley Project threw a little water and a great deal of electrical power at many consumers to enlist their support, but primarily it was, in design and rationale, a faucet for irrigation farmers.

Donald Worster, historian, 1985

Today, irrigation keeps crops green where once grasses browned, but in those increasingly remote and shrinking places where some semblance of the original botanical community can be found, spring brings a kaleidoscopic array of wild-flowers, then summer bleaches all to hay, and it remains that way until the next spring. It is on just such soil that irrigation has produced riches.

But irrigation may be a mixed blessing. The pumping of groundwater, for example, has caused the valley's floor to sink—land subsidence, geologists call it—so that today many residents of the San Joaquin actually live and work over thirty feet lower than the Indians who preceded them. Another neg-ative result of irrigation is salinity: the occurrence of various salts in soil or water in concentrations that interfere with agri-cultural growth; more than 400,000 acres of farmland are now affected by salts. And these are only two high-profile problems.

California, like many other areas of irrigated agriculture, continues to manage its soil and water systems as if there will be no day of judgment. . . . It is projected that by the turn of the century, in just sixteen years, another million acres could be lost to salinity.

Lowell N. Lewis, director, Agricultural Experiment
Station, University of California, 1984

Land subsidence in the San Joaquin Valley . . . represents one of the great changes man has imposed on the environment. About 5,200 square miles of irrigable land, one-half the entire valley, has been affected by subsidence, and maximum subsidence exceeded twenty-eight feet in 1970 . . .

J.F. Poland, B.E. Lofgren, R.L. Ireland,
& R.G. Pugh, geologists, 1972

I believe that introduced annual plants may prevent many perennial grasses from attaining their dominance, that annuals are now a large part of the climax on many sites (if not all of it), and that alien species should be considered as new and permanent members of the grassland rather than as aliens. Their elimination from the California prairie is inconceivable.

Harold F. Heady, botanist, 1977

On the valley's level surface, perennial bunchgrass was the major cover. Across the grasslands, three large ruminants roamed: pronghorn antelope and tule elk were lowland natives, and they were joined by mule deer that grazed down from the foothills. The former are entirely gone from their valley range, while elk roam only small reserves; deer remain common on the valley's edges. The ruminants were prey for an abundance of grizzly bears. More challenging and more conspicuous than beavers or elk, grizzlies were doomed; wrote Henry Henshaw in 1876, "Perhaps few animals have suffered more from persistent and relentless warfare waged by man than this formidable bear." None has been seen in the valley since the last century, leaving humans as the area's most dangerous predators.

Other predators once swam above the valley's floor. Thick marine sediments reveal that an ancient sea covered the region before the mountains rose, and even today sharks' teeth are dug up. "Maximum thickness of (marine) sediments in the Great Valley is more than ten miles," writes Oakeshott. "The present flat floor . . . has been built up by sediments deposited by streams and shallow lakes during the last million years or so." As a Yokuts creation tale has it, "Once there was a time when there was nothing in the world but water . . ." Once the water was gone and the Yokuts settled, they did so with an intimacy unknown to the Europeans who would displace them.

My words are tied in one
with the great mountains,
With the great rocks,
with the great trees,
In one with my body
and in my heart . . .
And you, day,
and you, night!
All of you see me
one with this world.

"A Prayer," Yokuts

The world with which the Yokuts were one was the Great Valley. They captured waterfowl, hunted elk and antelope, harvested grasses and seeds, for they were the most numerous of the region's native dwellers, but there was diversity of human population, with four major tribes—all members of the Penutian language family—dominant: Wintu and Maidu inhabited the north; Yokuts dwelled in the south; Miwoks separated north and south with a relatively small east-central intrusion. Alfred Kroeber called the valley "the Penutian Empire," and the Penutians understood well their relationship to nature:

Thunder and Lightning are two great spirits who try to destroy mankind. But Rainbow is a good spirit who speaks gently to them, and persuades them to let the Indians live a little longer.

"Thunder and Lightning," Maidu

California's heartland boasted one of the densest native populations in North America, nearly 160,000 according to high estimates. "Here were to be found most of her (California's) Indians," writes Theodora Kroeber, "the predominant physical type, and the carriers of the most idiosyncratic culture. Three hundred tribelets of California's five hundred or more belong to this area." Living in an area that, according to their own oral histories, had never suffered a famine, valley Indians were considered wealthy and peaceful.

He-who-is-above planted different acorn trees, different berries, different clovers; he put fish in the rivers, he made all kinds of animals for the Wintu.

All Indian tribes increased all over this island. There were no whites.

"He-Who-Is-Above," Wintu

The figure and form of these Indians is graceful; both men and women are taller than ordinary. The men have the custom of smearing their heads in the form of a cross (the efficacy and mysteries of which are yet unknown to them) with white mud.

Captain Pedro Fages, explorer, 1775

The Europeans who began entering the valley in the late eighteenth century were less wealthy and considerably less peaceful than the Indians they found here. In March, 1772, a party that included Captain Pedro Fages and Fray Juan Crespi climbed a spur of Mount Diablo and beheld "a plain as level as the palm of the hand," according to Crespi, ". . . all level land as far as the eye could see." They had discovered something unusual indeed for, as Bakker explains, "There is no other flat area of comparable size west of the Rockies." Moreover, the Spaniards also noted another distinct characteristic of the terrain, a river so wide that Crespi claimed it was the "largest that has been discovered in New Spain."

29 the March N 6 Miles and encamp on river. i was obliged to cross many Slous of the River that were verry miry and passed great numbers of indians who were engaged in digging Roots. I succeeded in giving to them some presents. they were small in size and apparently verry poor and miserable. The most of them had little Rbit Skin Robes. 11 Beaver taken.

Jedediah Strong Smith, trapper
(journal entry, 1828)

The Spanish did not settle the valley, but Americans did trickle in, trappers like Jedediah Smith mostly, but some settlers too such as John Bidwell, John Marsh and John Sutter, until 1849 and the Gold Rush, when it became a place to hurry through in order to reach the diggings. It also became a larder; commercial hunters decimated waterfowl as well as large mammals: deer, antelope, elk. In its naturally irrigated regions, produce was grown; more importantly, an imported, domesticated grass, wheat, was dry farmed and within fifteen years of the Gold Rush, the valley had become one of the nation's great grain-producing regions. However, it was not until the coming of the railroad and the development of sophisticated irrigation that the agriculture burgeoned and farming communities grew.

The great reapers were drawn by thirty mules, moving like an army through the square miles of waving wheat. Threshing crews worked from sunup to dark, their cooks even longer; and the mountains of chaff rose high enough, it seemed, to tower above the Sutter Buttes. On both the Sacra-

*mento and San Joaquin Rivers, barges or shallow draft,
"dew skimming" steamers took the golden grain down the
rivers to the bay, which led to the world beyond.*

W.H. Hutchinson, historian, 1980

*Standing at the edge of our city, a man could feel that we had
made this place of streets and dwellings in the stillness and
loneliness of the desert, and we had done a brave thing. We
had come to this dry area that was without history, and we
had paused in it and built our houses and we were slowly
creating the legend of our life. We were digging for water and
we were leading streams through the dry land. We were
planting and ploughing and standing in the midst of the
garden we were making.*

William Saroyan, writer, 1934

*It's a countryside created by enterprising landowners who
carved fields from ancient lake beds, rearranged the river
system of California and relied increasingly on deadly
chemicals.*

*Sooner or later the water and chemicals would come
together . . .*

Lynn Ludlow, reporter, 1985

Today, agriculture and the valley are virtually synony-
mous. Although two centuries ago, most of its land would have
been considered semi-desert, it is now the richest agricultural
region on earth, producing more than 200 crops, 25 percent of
all table foods consumed in the United States. As Hutchinson
points out, "No other economic sector in the state so directly
affects every Californian; . . . No other . . . occupies so much
land; uses so many natural resources; involves so many people
in the food chain . . . yet seems so much to be taken for
granted."

The next time someone mentions that boring drive along I-5 linking the two Californias, just remind them they are crossing a facet of one of the absolute jewels of western civilization.

Garrison Sposito, environmental scientist, 1985

Fifty or sixty years ago one farmer produced enough food for five or six other people. Now one farmer produces enough food for fifty or sixty people, and you're not going to do that with your hands on a shovel.

Jack Stone, farmer, 1984

The vast natural watershed of the Sierra Nevada makes possible the abundance of valley agriculture for, in combination with the region's rich soil and climate, it has produced even beyond the dreams of its developers. But a fourth ingredient has also been necessary: labor. Hard work and people willing to do it characterize the valley. An anonymous ballad from the 1870s sums up the toil:

Don't go, I say, if you've got any brains,
You'll stay far away from the San Joaquin plains.
At four in the morning they're hustling up tools,
Feed, curry and harness ten long-eared old mules.
Plow twenty-four miles through sunshine and rain,
Or your blankets you'll roll on the San Joaquin plain.

The availability of work has attracted to this area a multi-ethnic cast of tenacious settlers willing to earn their survival with hard physical labor.

Chinese, Japanese, Southern European, East Indian, Mexican, Filipino, Okie, Black—wave after wave of people providing migrant labor in order to claw their way up the socio-economic ladder—have migrated to this flat territory; the result is a rigorously heterogenous culture, marred at times by xenophobia and racism, but remarkably free from the sweeps and swoops of coastal trendiness. The ready availability of laborers has, unfortunately, led some growers—especially those with massive, corporate holdings that dominate valley farming—to consider it, like cheap water, their due, and that has often resulted in an insensitivity to the needs of migrant workers.

The farm labor problem of California is undoubtedly the worst in the United States. It is bad for the farmers themselves, and worse, if possible, for those whom they employ. In many respects, it is even worse than old-time slavery.

> *San Francisco Morning Chronicle*
> September 5, 1875

No matter how familiar one may be with "rural" California, it is always rather surprising to note the manners and appearance of the gentry who step forward to speak in the name of "the farmers" at legislative hearings in Sacramento. These men are "operators" not "farmers."

> Carey McWilliams, historian, 1949

"It's never popular to be poor—only in the Bible," he said. "A man must have invented stoop labor because a snake never would."

> Chester Seltzer, writer, 1969

Agriculture is, of course, not the only industry in the Great Central Valley, but it dominates both the image and reality of the region. Despite the fact that, suicidally it seems, the region loses thousands of farm acres each year, despite the fact that it now boasts perhaps the fastest-growing population in the state, despite the fact that many small towns have been engulfed by its growing cities, the valley nonetheless remains a rural area, one that retains cultural values unglossed by the sudden sophistication of urban life. Turn on the radio and you'll hear music not apt to be piped into an elevator—Mexican rancheros or traditional country. Look around and you'll see more dark faces with white foreheads—or dark faces with dark foreheads—than stylish tans. Listen carefully and you'll hear many languages other than English and Spanish: Tagalog, Basque, Sikh, Laotian, and Yokuts among many others. While some residents certainly succumb to passing fashions and gaze longingly at coastal cities, they tend in fact not to be people who work the soil but those who indirectly gain income from it.

And there's another thing: an excellent labor supply here. People are steady, hard working, very little turnover. Something about these people here, they give a day's work for a day's pay.

> John Sommerhalder, division head,
> Tenneco West, 1984

The small owner's landscape is a scattered, localized one, clustering at the edges of towns, where jobs are available. . . . The landscape of big ownership stretches all around the small holdings, a sea in which the waves are arranged in orderly, dirt brown rows.

> David Rains Wallace, writer, 1984

"Outside the towns," writes James D. Houston, "it is still a land of pickup trucks and horse trailers and hay bales, a land of row crops and cattle herds, with vast rice fields in the north and walking beams that sprout from oil fields in the far south." And those elements contribute mightily to the particular *sense* of valley life that many natives retain even after education and employment have deposited them elsewhere. Unless they were part of that tiny, elite caste protected from tule fog and summer sun by the comforts of wealth, they will have confronted nature. The area's poets touch a core:

The fog, that nightlong had lain to the fields,
Earth-loving, lifted at noon, broke to no wind,
Sheeted the sky blue-gray and deadened.

The sun somewhere over the dark height ran steeply
down west;
And that hour, silence hanging the wide and naked
vineyards,
The fog fell slowly with twilight, masking the land.

William Everson, Selma

Late November: a sixty-knot
squall through Carquinez
Strait breaks
levees, backs salt water miles
inland to preserve
what it kills . . .

Dennis Schmitz, Sacramento

In our ditch
there are water skaters,
frogs,
tall reeds,
mud bugs,
apple cores and plum seeds,
and little naked children.

Khatchik Minasian, Fresno

In the wild rice fields two rivers
meet;
one river from the north bears soil
so fertile that the dead
grow
in their graves.
The other carried the cleaned bones
and empty skin
of animals that once lived
inside the mountain snows . . .

Gary Thompson, Chico

Winter,
infiltrator of soft linings
perfect tooth of stone,
thief of horses
and children . . .
When we call, our voices
turn and come meekly
back to us.

Roberta Spear, Hanford

They are varied voices from a varied place where once elk and antelope roamed, where grizzlies prowled and marshes hid legions of red-wing blackbirds, where primeval riparian forests were erogenous zones for lovers intent on secret rendezvous. Today at least some of its land is toxic, a byproduct of scientific farming. Like the rest of California, it is beginning to evidence the ravages of overpopulation. With all its apparent open space, the valley is vulnerable: it cannot feed the nation if it is paved; it cannot provide water from contaminated wells; it cannot grow crops in poisoned soil.

Still, in the face of evidence of slow deterioration, the valley retains a stark, sometimes deceptive beauty—here desolate, there verdant. Concern about human exploitation of the region is well-founded. But nature is resilient; people may fill the valley and abuse it, but nature controls the water, the soil, the weather. How much more human manipulation can this land endure? People must understand and work within nature's constraints lest the biological tragedy at Kesterson Reservoir become but the first visible stage of a downward spiral here in the golden state's heartland.

More recent observations by experts are that the dangerous
waste product is menacing wildlife in the largest expanses of
the grasslands districts in the valley—a far bigger territory
than Kesterson. Birds are being found with selenium levels
resembling or exceeding those found in Kesterson wildlife.

Editorial, *San Francisco Examiner*
June 23, 1985

Nonetheless, on summer afternoons when the sun begins to slip beyond the Coast Ranges and the frequently polluted sky hovers dangerously on the cusp of red, irrigators lean against their shovels and gaze westward across textured croplands, wrinkled rows in soil shadowed by clods, certain that this their reality is sufficient. But those men and women of the land tend not to perceive the larger pattern: the place Sposito identifies as "the most productive agricultural area in the history of the world" continues to be manipulated, possibly maimed. The old vaquero, Arnold Rojas, who has lived here for three-quarters of a century, sees things clearly: "Some day we will have to plow up the malls to plant something we can eat."

REFLECTIONS ON
CALIFORNIA'S REGIONALISM   [1985]

During the interminable discussions that finally led a committee—beleaguered if not benighted—to approve the volume of stories that constituted half of my doctoral dissertation, I absorbed a good-natured barb from one unimpressed prof: "Who cares what happens in the sticks?" The answer was simple: I did.

I still do. I care because I'm from the sticks and I know that what happens there is what happens in life, all life. The setting and subjects of those tales seemed to bother him more than their questionable quality, and I've come to suspect that had some of them been set in a university club in San Francisco rather than a honky tonk in Modesto he might have found them more acceptable. Personally, I think both places are fine and, of course, both are California.

Thinking about that experience the other day brought to mind an essay by Don Graham in the *Texas Humanist*, an essay in which he responded to an assertion that Houston—with its glut of imported writers—had become the hub of Texas letters. Graham borrowed and modified Phillip Rahv's terminology and declared that such outsiders were "paleface" writers, the literacy equivalent of white wine and fern bars. He went on to say that he preferred "redskin" authors, those bred and born on Texas soil and probably still scraping souvenirs of ranch life from their souls as well as their soles: Elmer Kelton and Rolando Hinojasa *si*, Phillip Lopate and Cynthia McDonald *no*.

California's redskin writers, in the tradition of Mark Twain rather than Henry James, have sweated here without shame, have lusted and fought and toiled here, and they acknowledge the good and bad and everything in between about this place. That does not, of course, make them better than palefaces, but it certainly makes them *different*.

18

California, as the nation's number one destination, as well as a vast, diverse state, has its share of both kinds and both have contributed to our literature: from Helen Hunt Jackson through Aldous Huxley to Herbert Gold, many a paleface has offered interesting commentary, as have the Jack Londons, John Steinbecks, and William Saroyans, redskins. This paleface/redskin dichotomy is, of course, only metaphoric, but in a state where two weeks of residence seems to create instant experts, it is useful. In fact, many of California's finest writers seem to combine elements of both: native born and blooded, then shaped by education and social complexity. Nearly all seem better when they achieve a tad of distance, too.

Looking back at my own life, for example, I must admit that my aesthetic sense, as well as my social taste, was in no small measure molded by that rich if raw province, the San Joaquin Valley, and that this occurred long before I knew universities and cities. You see, I was born and raised at the southern end of the valley in a little town called Oildale. I was married there and one of my children was born there—the one said to be most like me, ironically. My feelings steeped in that valley and still resonate there. By the time I thought about being a valley boy, I had already been one for nearly thirty years, so to a degree at least, I'm a redskin.

When *do* you become aware of your place? Long before you become conscious of it, certainly. Awareness, like the autonomic system, functions independent of and more vitally than consciousness. It records, it stores and, if you are lucky, at some distant point you may open an artistic channel to those riches; Lawrence Clark Powell suggests that regional writers must tap "the deep unconscious sources on which literature feeds. They reach down to the subsoil of feeling that lies far beneath the topsoil of thinking." William Carlos Williams goes further when he asserts that good writing comes from "the shape of men's lives imparted by the places where they have experience. . . . The locale is the only thing that is universal." While grandest human dramas can happen any place, they must happen *some* place, and good writers recognize that fact. California offers world enough and time.

In a recent essay, "One Can Think About Life After The Fish Is In The Canoe," James D. Houston contrasts what he calls Old Provincialism with New Regionalism. The former, he defines as a "stubborn attachment to the only place one really knows." The latter, on the other hand, "is regionalism at a higher level of awareness about the interlocking and interdependent workings of the world," requiring distance and perspective as well as understanding and acceptance. These are important distinctions, since Houston is himself a major California writer with more than a hint of red skin.

When as an apprentice I began to write for publication, I set my stories in Paris (where I'd never been) or San Francisco (which I didn't understand). That was a long time ago. By now I've visited Paris and lived in San Francisco, but I write about the San Joaquin Valley. I do so because, if I have one, it is my window onto the universal, the archetypal, the significant. Its subjects are more than sufficient and its people embody for me the human condition.

What has all this to do with teaching English? I am not unique in being a native Californian who employs local settings to explore issues minor or grand. If I were developing a literature program in this state, especially for a secondary school, I would start by teaching local or nearby redskins who write about recognizable experiences and places, and use such work to hook youngsters on reading, then move students toward classics. If offering, for example, a course in Sacramento, I would begin with the work of authors such as Jose Montoya, Joan Didion, Dennis Schmitz, and Richard Rodriguez, four accomplished writers who in at least some of their art explore the state capital and its environs. Next I would employ a regional ripple, introducing other important authors from the Great Central Valley, then from the state, the nation, the world, in that sequence. I would employ the power of the familiar in literature to create readers who might later be led to Shakespeare and Cervantes, Mishima and Borges.

But doesn't using local material somehow limit the scope available? It could, if no writers of quality have developed in a given area, but all writing is finally set in some place at some time. The question of universality of power hinges more on an artist's talent and craft than on an area's limitations. While there are those who argue that the ruminations of an individual wrestling his or her conscience in Manhattan are intrinsically more important than those of someone doing the same thing in the Santa Cruz Mountains, they are wrong; it is likely that they have been duped by the absurd, if hoary, belief that somehow eastern American experience is national, while everything else is "only" regional. Obviously, our nation's tradition *is* regional because our nation is composed of regions. What matters finally is a writer's genius in the use of material.

Place, itself, can be a vital factor in the savor of art, and no comparable area of the United States offers more diversity than California. Contemporary illusions concerning this state are largely the product of misunderstanding fostered by mass media that proclaim their own glittering versions of Southern California to be this state's homogeneous reality. In fact, this varied series of places, multi-ethnic since earliest settlement, and lumped together under one name, offers writers a startling variety of subjects, situations, and settings.

Four geo-literary regions have emerged in writing from the Golden State, each reflecting specific characteristics such as patterns of settlement, population, landscapes, ethnotypes, economies and social milieus. Two are obvious: the North Coast and Southern California.

The former extends from Big Sur north toward Oregon, with the San Francisco-Oakland Bay Area its core. In no other place has the East more dramatically penetrated and influenced the West. From Gold Rush immigrants such as Alonzo Delano and George Horatio Derby, through the Golden Gate Trinity (Ina Coolbrith, Bret Harte, Charles Warren Stoddard) and their associate Mark Twain, including Bohemias in San Francisco, Piedmont, Carmel and such singulars as Jack London, Gertrude Atherton, and Joaquin Miller, right up to the Beats of the 1950s and the Hippies of the 1960s and 70s, this has historically been considered the state's most significant literary area.

Southern California, dominated by the San Diego-Los Angeles freeway culture, was until late in the nineteenth century the wild west. Called "the Cow Counties," its literary life really began in 1884 when Helen Hunt Jackson's *Ramona* created a mythic history on which later developers built. And they weren't the only ones, since much of the southland's writing seems linked to myths of one kind or another; it has, for example, been the locus of more than 2,000 novels dealing with Hollywood and moviemaking. Perhaps its most important contribution has been the perfection of the detective novel, which was originally developed by Dashiell Hammett on the North Coast. In the hands of Raymond Chandler, James M. Cain, and Ross MacDonald, it was not a novelty but a unique response to unyielding modern realities. Today authors such as Charles Bukowski, Wanda Coleman, Ron Koertge, Kate Braverman and Gerald Locklin produce experimental work of high quality there.

The Great Central Valley has long been dismissed by some urban commentators as a local version of the Great American Desert—in part because it is viewed as redskin territory. Yet artists have for a long time recognized its power: Frank Norris set *The Octopus* there; Mary Austin began writing there; John Steinbeck's Joads settled there. In the 1930s, two significant locals, William Saroyan and William Everson emerged, and writers have been emerging ever since, especially writers of the soil: Luis Valdez, Leonard Gardner, Maxine Hong Kingston, Larry Leavis, William Rintoul, Richard Dokey, Gary Soto, Wilma Elizabeth McDaniel, Frank Bidart, plus the aforementioned Sacramento writers; the list could go on and on. In point of fact, a strong case can be made that the valley is the most productive and interesting literary region in contemporary California.

The fourth geo-literary region evidenced in this state's literature is an abstraction, Wilderness California: deserts, mountains, undeveloped woodlands and coastlands. It was here that the literary reclamation of the desert occurred, a move sparked by John C. Van Dyke and Mary Hunter Austin. It was here that John Muir, Clarence King, George M. Stewart, Walter Van Tilburg Clark and Gary Snyder wrote of the Sierra.

It was here that Robinson Jeffers used the wild coast to symbolize the universe, here that David Rains Wallace used the Klamath reaches to reconsider evolution.

Another kind of wilderness typifies a fifth region, this one nongeographic but definitely literary: Fantasy California. It is the most intriguing and most abstract of the state's literary areas, a subjective realm that explores not real people and places but the gap between what people—especially palefaces—expect and what they find. California has always been as much state of mind as state of the union. In Fantasy California, the stereotype rules: sun-bleached blondes on roller skates exchange high fives while hurrying to hot tubs after toiling in their marijuana patches. Deanna Durbin and Robert Paige sang in a 1945 movie:

> The climate is better
> The ocean is wetter
> The mountains are higher
> The deserts are drier
> The hills have more splendor
> The girls have more gender
> Ca-li-for-ni-ay!

Such hyperbole leads to fanciful expectations; as a result, work both illusioned and disillusioned has been produced, from the Gold Rush disappointment of Alonzo Delano (" . . . the greatness of California! Faugh!") to such fascinating volumes as Evelyn Waugh's *The Loved One*, Robert Roper's *Royo County*, Ernest Callenbach's *Ecotopia*, and Cyra McFadden's *The Serial*.

Fantasy California's greatest expression is Nathaniel West's *The Day of the Locust*. Californiaphobes assert that West's novel epitomizes the Golden State. In fact it reveals the state of West's mind and his view of the human condition. He wrote to Josephine Herbst after he had moved to Hollywood to become a screenwriter:

> This place is Asbury Park, New Jersey. . . . In other words, phooey on Cal. Another thing, this stuff about easy work is all wrong. My hours are from ten in the morning to six at night with a full day on Saturdays. There's no fooling here.

"Cal" turned out to be a real place with "no fooling here," not the wonderland he had expected, so a chasm between expectation and reality yawned. That chasm is the setting of *The Day of the Locust*.

This concept of regions should be seen as an acknowledgement of this state's diversity and richness rather than an iron-clad dictum. As Houston comments, California "is really a large mosaic of regions, each with its singular identity and microclimate." Those of us who live here recognize that there is more than one California.

We also know that the old saw which suggests that the Golden State is full of nuts is really a backhanded compliment, for it is a recognition of one of its best features: its tolerance of individual variation. Even in my rural province, I learned to accept human variety because I rubbed elbows with bearded prophets and wizened mystics, with Mexican revolutionaries and Okie rebels, and I grew up considering ethnically mixed marriages unexceptional. Moreover, many in my generation, myself included, evidence another California reality, the upward social and economic mobility predicated by our state's remarkable educational system. California produced Richard Nixon and Joan Baez, Earl Warren and Cesar Chavez, Jerry Brown and Jerry Garcia. And look at the non-natives who've been shaped here: Ronald Reagan and Tom Bradley, S. I. Hayakawa and Marilyn Monroe. We live in a rigorously heterogeneous place and I, for one, love it.

Having been born in California seems to me to have been great good fortune. I'm especially happy to have been raised where and when I was, because my life stretches from the Great Depression to what I call the Great Expression, today's burst of creative activity. I've lived all over, but always return to the valley that spawned me. Occasionally well-intended friends will suggest that I write about other places and other people, expand my vistas as it were. What they don't understand is that as a beginner I tried, but when I rejected my feeling and went elsewhere in my work, I found that the valley grasped my organs like tree roots entwining rocks, wound around and through them so that it was difficult to tell if one existed independent of the other. I am the things that made me: the soil, the society, the experiences. We all are. That is why consequential art *must* be particular in order to be universal.

Let me repeat my contention that there is no place that cannot produce significant writing. Some outsiders assert that life in California is too easy, thus the state cannot temper artists properly, but they actually reveal more about their own inaccurate notions of where and what we are than about us. Those commentators have never chopped cotton beneath the searing weight of central valley sun, have never drilled for oil in that region's frigid and engulfing tule fog, have never grubbed through garbage cans, fighting other luckless people for the leftovers of affluence. Those are California realities too.

Wallace Stegner recently observed: "There is every sort of richness, every sort of quality, in California, to counteract a fairly pervasive vulgarity. No richness and no quality should go unreported, and the merely sensational doesn't need to be hyped." Some of California's writers need to be redskins, or the state's reality will pass unnoticed.

We can discuss this all day, but I think Stegner makes essentially the same point I do: know your place as it really is and write honestly of it. If your talent is sufficient, the place certainly will be. It is not my suggestion that California's pale-face writers be avoided—they proliferate here and are a legitimate reflection of what we are—but that you don't avoid the redskins. Recognize both and give the state's heterogeneity the credit it deserves. After all, that rich mix *is* California.

THE OKIES:
FORTY YEARS LATER [1975]

Today they are state legislators and used-car salesmen, waitresses and college professors; they are convicts, guards, country music impresarios, construction workers and contractors, farm laborers and winos; they are, in a word, Californians. But those Okies who struggled into this not-always-golden state during the 1930s have not forgotten the days when an official in Madera said of them: "The squatter is usually . . . nothing more or less than an idler and a parasite on the body politic of the people surrounding them. They are a burden on the taxpayer and the growers . . ."

"Them thangs hurt," recalls Lemuel Bundy, "but they helped too. I know they made me sore and I just determined we'd make'er." Make'er the Okies have, yet scars from those painful, sometimes desperate days occasionally hover near the surface of the original migrants, as well as their progeny. In central California most any old boy can still get his features altered right quick if he calls someone "Okie" in the wrong tone, for the word remains a popular expression of derision in some contexts: siphon hoses used to steal gas are called Okie credit cards; the worst calves in a herd are called Okies. Use of the term has been traced back to 1905, and Ben Reddick of the *Los Angeles Times* is usually credited (or blamed) for having popularized it during the 1930s. Today some Oklahomans both misunderstand and resent the term as meaning "depression drifters."

The actual migrants were of course a heterogeneous collection; mostly, though not all, white. While Oklahoma was the focus of attention, they drifted west from across the Great Plains and rural South; the Dakotas, Nebraska, Kansas, Missouri, Oklahoma, Mississippi, Texas, New Mexico and Arkansas. In the old days, "Texie" and "Arkie" were also common terms, but as time passed, nearly all migrants came to be called Okies once they had reached California. In the 1960s, Dewey Bartlett, then Governor of Oklahoma, tried to improve the word's connotation, but with little luck. However, contemporary achievements, along with the younger generation's growing understanding of what their elders survived, have effected the improvement.

A stubborn, deep pride has grown. Paul Westmoreland, known throughout central California as "Okie Paul," sums it up: "To me, Okies are anyone who went through the period like we did, whether they're from Oklahoma or Illinios or Texas. Okies are anyone who picked that cotton for 50¢ a hundred pounds, or picked potatoes for 15¢ an hour."

If the people were heterogeneous, so were the forces that led them to migrate. Although the Dust Bowl was but a small portion of the area from which they came, it is understandable that the massive dust storms should be popularly identified as the migration's cause, for they were both highly visible and dramatic. The major causes of the migration, all interrelated, as traced by Walter Stein in *California and the Dust Bowl Migration*, were rural poverty; tenant farming practices; mechanization of farming; drought; New Deal crop curtailment policies; soil depletion and depression.

A general rural poverty intensified the other pressures. Recalls Mrs. Frances Walker, who lives now in Keyes, California: "In Oklahoma one year I carried (walked) my two-year-old daughter a mile and half to pick cotton, with our lunch and my cotton-pick sack. I bought my oldest kids clothes, and I averaged 85¢ a day. It bought our clothes and a couple of blankets for our beds." Midwest and Southwestern farm people were charged high railroad rates that made shipping their produce to markets barely profitable; further, recurrent droughts created an unstable economic pattern that often made them victims of high bank interest rates. Naturally, the large numbers of folk dependent upon farmers for their livelihood—tenants, laborers, tradespeople, shopkeepers—were profoundly affected by the same problems; they, in fact, formed the bulk of the migrants.

27

When they finally moved, folks tended to drift west along parallel lines—migrants from the northern plains moved to the Pacific Northwest; California's great length gathered people from the middle and southern plains. In all more than 500,000 people trekked west; some 350,000 settled in California. In addition to its vast corporate agricultural industry, California's reputation as the promised land attracted Okies.

Later research had invalidated the once popular idea that Okies came to California because of the state's "overly liberal" welfare program. Except in 1938, a year of disastrous floods coupled with crop curtailments, Okies strongly resisted welfare. Only in February, a month when there was little or no work in the fields, would welfare rolls shoot up. In fact, self-help became ever more the rule during hard times; it was John Steinback's Ma Joad in *The Grapes of Wrath* who said it most clearly: "I'm learnin' one thing good," she said, "learnin' it all atime, ever' day. If you're in trouble or hurt or need—go to poor people. They're the only ones that'll help—the only ones." Recalls Flossie Haggard, mother of country singer, Merle:

> I remember we broke down in the middle of the desert. We were out of water, and just when I thought we weren't going to make it, I saw this boy coming down the highway on a bicycle. He was going all the way from Kentucky to Fresno. He shared a quart of water with us and helped fix the car. Everybody'd been treating us like trash, and I told this boy, "I'm glad to see there's still some decent folks left in this world." He rode the rest of the way with us, and I still write him. (Paul Hemphill, the *Atlantic Monthly*, September 1971.)

Historians have also dismissed the widely held belief that handbills put out by California growers lured most Okies to the state. Like the welfare notion, there is a kernel of truth in the handbill theory. Some California growers did circulate them, as did unscrupulous labor contractors, but more evidence points at Arizona growers seeking Okies. The following advertisement appeared in the *Daily Oklahoman* on October 13, 1937:

> Cotton pickers. Several thousand still wanted to arrive here before November 15th; growers paying 85¢ short staple ... houses or tents free; ideal climate ... Farm Labor Service, 28 West Jefferson, Phoenix, Ariz.

Growers hired Okies to chop and pick Arizona cotton, which matured earlier than California's, then encouraged them to move on. A *New York Times* reporter called it "the neatest get rich scheme of the century," for Arizonans got their share of the Okies' work, but few of the headaches the influx brought.

And there were headaches. Within rural California, the migrants' desire to settle as quickly as possible went against the state's traditional migratory labor pattern and raised many hackles in the small towns favored by the Okies. An article in the January 13, 1937, *Mid-Week Pictorial* noted that the migrants' ambition was "to get settled down ... where they can pick cotton and send children to school." So strong was the nesting instinct that it was not uncommon for an Okie family to establish residence even while the father, and often the mother too, continued following the crops until a stable job could be found. The family came first—especially the children—and Okies recognized early that education offered the best hope of escape from poverty, though many came to misunderstand and hate the changes it wrought in their children.

It was in education and its related social sphere that Okies most threatened locals. The agricultural areas in which most migrants settled were poorly equipped to assimilate large numbers of newcomers, and some rural counties received whopping numbers indeed; Kern, for example, took in 52,554, a 63.6 percent population increase between 1935 and 1940. In that same agonizing period, especially from 1938 on, groups such as the California State Chamber of Commerce helped stir anti-migrant sentiments, hinting that the migrants, among other things, were sexual degenerates (and hinting at the same time that they were unusually effective sexually).

During the 1940s and 1950s, the children of many of the same Californians who most feared and hated Okies found themselves attracted to the children of the migrants. After all, they had been raised on stories of Okie licentiousness, so why not find out for themselves? Many a frowned-upon marriage resulted. There was still another unforeseen complication, one that remains rarely discussed: Okies were white people doing traditionally nonwhite work; their ambivalent racial position allowed them to date nonwhites, especially Mexicans, and that contributed in no small measure to realignment of social relationships.

Okies today are still split on racial matters. Most oldtimers remain relatively unchanged in their orientation, though their rhetoric is more fierce than their actions, for the harshness of survival taught them the folly of inflexibility. Among their kids more diversity is evident: some participate in groups like Kern County's erstwhile White Citizens' Council, once reputed to be America's largest outside the Deep South; others have learned from mutual misery that only understanding and respect can help America: an Okie college professor initiated one of the state's most efficient minority recruitment programs and most highly respected ethnic studies curriculums, while Merle Haggard, the powerful Okie bard, has reflected in songs like "Irma Jackson" and "White Man Singin' the Blues" an enlighted and compassionate vision. Most Okies, however, like most other Californians, do nothing one way or another.

Politically and economically, the coming of the Okies was deeply resented. During their poverty years, the migrants did indeed find themselves forced to use county health, education and relief facilities, while adding little to tax income. In those same hard years, they tended to be either Midwestern Populists or Southern Democrats, and California was a Republican state. In 1938, when Culbert Olson defeated incumbent Governor Frank Merriam, conservatives howled. They found Okies easy scapegoats for their defeat. More recently Haggard's "Okie from Muskogee" has rattled liberal and radical cages, and resulted in overgeneralized claims about reactionary Okie politics. Yet here, too, generalizations are difficult.

Although Merle Haggard's name is perhaps more closely identified with "Okie music" nationally, the resourceful Buck Owens, a superb entertainer himself, dominates "Music City West" (Bakersfield, that is). And Bakersfield is the heart of Kern County, where Route 66 directed migrants into the lush San Joaquin Valley; it is also the heart of traditional country music, closer to the non-orchestrated past than Nashville itself. Along with Owens, Haggard and Dallas Frazier, such stars as Tommy Collins, Freddie Hart, Lefty Frizzell, Bonnie Owens, Billy Mize, Bill Woods, Buddy Alan, Susan Raye and the late Don Rich are identified with what is proudly called the capital of the Okie sound.

Country music is important on another level, for Okie culture tended to be oral/aural, with singing bards and tellers of tales its indigenous literary people. Where then does Oklahoma's Woody Guthrie stand? His fame grew among intellectual sympathizers, not migrant Okies; surveys conducted in the San Joaquin Valley in the past two years indicate that Woody is far better known in Berkeley's salons than in Bakersfield's saloons. Still, like John Steinbeck, Guthrie remains a masterful interpreter of a time and place that suited his special talents.

Social protest and union activities were two other areas of Okie activity that greatly concerned conservative Californians during the bad old days. Few of the Okies who struggled west joined the attempts to organize California farm laborers during the late 1930s. The United Cannery, Agricultural, Packing, and Allied Workers of America (UCAPAWA), a CIO union, had little appeal for Okie supporters because, by 1938-39, most migrants were in desperate straits, often near starvation, sunk to a level where bare survival, especially for their children, obviated any theoretical economic concerns. The CIO was then often called a Red union, and one migrant summed up his feelings when he said: "We got enough troubles without going Communist." Walter Stein has documented that "Okies played a larger role as strikebreakers than as strikers."

It really isn't surprising—though it may be disappointing—that Okies, given their ambivalent racial attitudes and past experience with agricultural unions, have not tended to support Cesar Chavez's struggle to organize farm laborers, or that they often parrot allegations about UFWOC's Red taint that sound remarkably like the attacks once launched against UCAPAWA. Most of the arguments used against UFWOC were honed during the 1930s. Ironically, many Okies today are union people who consider Chavez's organization a maverick group.

Contemporary Okie political views, to the extent to which they can be generalized, are not unlike their views of organized labor: among older Okies there is little change from the Southern one-party view and the Midwestern Populism they brought with them. Their children are, by and large, Californians, though momma and daddy's background still makes itself felt. In the view of many Okies, the Democratic Party has moved too far to the Left, so that the American Independent Party's Populism is increasingly attractive now that Republican traditionalism has shown its warts. Withal, their thrust is conservative in most matters, reactionary in some, liberal in spots. Party labels, as is general in California politics, seem less important than specific, sometimes parochial, issues.

Within California's rapidly changing, trendy society, Okies have exerted a tempering, though spicy influence like the country cooking they favor, still retaining strong family ties, clannishness, traditional sex roles, sometimes absurd rites of passage, church affiliations, and a belief in America's promise (for they are proof that, however raggedly, it can be fulfilled). The work ethic has never faltered; "We've always known how to work," observes Okie Paul. "Gawd Almighty did we work. Had to or starve."

Then there is the agrarian myth: despite life in stucco suburbs and in growing cities like Fresno and Bakersfield, not to mention the sprawl of greater Los Angeles, many urban Okies retain rural values, perpetuating the cherished American illusion that we are a nation of yeoman farmers. "When you're urbanized you have to live by the rules," points out Karl Cozad, a Yuba County official whose parents were migrants. "They (Okies) want a little bigger piece of the ground." Perhaps in tacit recognition of the enduring strengths of such values, contemporary Okies try to retain at least symbolic contact with the "soil and soul," as Buck Owens has observed.

And many Okies have lived to see the externals of their traditions become part of California's current vogue; an Okie college professor, raised on the music of Bob Wills, Bill Woods, and Cousin Herb Henson, tells of having been visited by a student garbed in fashionably faded overalls who, observing the prof's record collection, exclaimed, "Wow! Are *you* into country?"

Most Okies remain into country, but as time passes they and their children are even more into California's crazy-quilt culture. If they have become enamored of trail bikes and color television sets and campers, their early poverty explains why. They are a tough, able, complex people who have given strong flavor to California's life. While they seem to have remained relatively static in racial and political matters, no group has struggled farther up the socio-economic ladder. Perfection is not an Okie characteristic, but a blues-like ability to accept adversity with grace and grit is. And they have not forgotten how to laugh at themselves.

In an often forgotten masterpiece of proletarian writing, *Their Blood Is Strong*, Steinbeck described life in a California ditch bank settlement:

> The three year old child has a gunny sack tied about his middle for clothing. He has the swollen belly caused by malnutrition.
> He sits on the ground in the sun in front of the house, and the little black fruit flies buzz in circles and land in his closed eyes and crawl up his nose until he weakly brushes them away . . .
> He will die in a very short time.

Surviving such hardships has given Okies a strong sense of their own endurance. Writes Frances Walker:

> The Okies were invincible, they won. They are here, they own land, homes, and are comfortable. Their children are here and their grandchildren. I'm part of it.

"Usta be," a college student recently admitted after studying the migrants' experiences, "you'd like hafta put slivers under my fingernails to make me tell that my folks're Okies. But now, well, I understand." Many people—Okies and non-Okies— have come to understand that the migration was an American epic. Time has softened much of its pain, and added perspective. One of Merle Haggard's songs best summarizes the migrants' current attitude: "I Take a Lot of Pride in What I Am."

WHO CAN WRITE WHAT? [1985]

Fifteen years ago, after reading in *Arizona Quarterly* a tale titled "Mala Torres," I wrote an admiring letter to its author. A week or so later, I received a note scrawled in pencil on a small, lined piece of paper torn from a pocket notebook. "I am happy that you like my story," it read. "I write my stories for pleasure when I am not working. I am an icer of boxcars here in El Paso." That was my introduction to Amado Jesus Muro.

Some years later, reading Katharine Newman's collection *American Ethnic Short Stories*, I was particularly impressed by Danny Santiago's "The Somebody." I didn't make personal contact with him until 1984 and, when I did, he was the subject of much controversy because major newspapers on both coasts had carried front-page stories revealing that he was not a young Chicano but, to quote the *San Francisco Examiner*, "73-year-old Dan James—Anglo, blacklisted, ex-Communist Party member, son of wealthy Missourians, graduate of Andover and Yale."

Like "Danny Santiago," "Amado Muro" had also been a *nom de plume*, although this was not revealed until after the death of Chester Seltzer in 1971. The persona who had written to me on notebook paper was as much an invention as "Mala Torres"; without realizing it, I had become part of Muro's fiction.

When I wrote to Dan James last year, I included a copy of an article about Muro/Seltzer. His response was refreshingly candid: "I note with amusement Muro's letter of 1970 which employs some of the dangling modifiers I tempted my agent with as Danny Santiago. . . . Believe me, Dan James was a major disappointment in the flesh to those who knew Danny from his letters." That was true, of course, because James is a journeyman writer; as such, he is neither as good as Danny Santiago was originally said to be by overcompensatory critics, nor as bad as has been suggested since his exposure. He writes as well now as ever and "The Somebody" remains as solid a piece of fiction as it ever was.

Although they never knew one another—or even *of* one another—Seltzer and James had much in common beyond literary gifts and the employment of Hispanic pen names. Much advocacy for the disadvantaged in American life smacks of elitism because it is dominated by the well-to-do, the well-educated, the well-intended. Both men fit that mold: they were maverick sons of prominent families, expensively educated (Seltzer studied with John Crow Ransome at Kenyon College) and both evidenced genuine commitment to America's down-trodden, especially poor Chicanos. It is important to add that both men originally employed Spanish pseudonyms in the early 1950s, when little advantage—save, perhaps, curiosity—accrued from a Hispanic name. They seem, in sum, products of a different time, victimized as much by their own empathy and by dramatically changing social conditions as by any personal failings. Still, Seltzer's and James' intentions are less important than their effects, so their uses of Latino names raise important issues and serve as a warning for future authors. The Muro/Seltzer and Santiago/James affairs are also interesting for what they reveal about America's literary subculture.

When convenient, literati confuse political and social values for aesthetic ones. As a result, a good story like "The Somebody" is called great by critics and scholars who are reading the author's Hispanic surname with greater intensity than the tale; moreover, folks in the know recognize the newly increased profit potential of a Spanish name. Proof that the former occurs requires only a survey of published reviews. The latter is more interesting: James explains that his agent suggested in the early 1970s that he expand "The Somebody" into a novel "since there was so little outlet"—read that as "so few big bucks"—for short stories. He complied and his agent "sent it around, but it was rejected everywhere." In 1981, his agent again offered it, and the manuscript, unaltered, was accepted by Simon and Schuster and published as *Famous All Over Town*.

Why? Had editors previously misread a masterpiece? Had it aged like fine cabernet in James' file? Most likely it was the continuing impact of outstanding novels by Chicano artists such as Rolando Hinojosa, Tomas Rivera, and Rudolfo Anaya, along with a maturing national interest in "ethnic" expression, that made *Famous All Over Town* such a potentially valuable property.

And valuable it turned out to be, winning the $5,000 Rosenthal Prize from the Institute of Arts and Letters. Moreover, it was rumored to be a strong candidate for the Pulitzer Prize, but the author would not submit the required biographical information so it could not be formally considered. After James' exposure, however, Arturo Islas asserted that the novel "has no literary merit." Presently, an "I-disliked-it-before-you-did" upmanship seems to be in effect, especially among Chicano scholars.

Asked Felipe de Ortego y Gasca, "If we are to judge *Famous All Over Town* on its own merits, not on the ancestry of the author, why was he not accessible?" The question, of course, need not be answered if we are to judge the novel on its own merits.

Ortego y Gasca, however, does answer and in a manner that suggests an important extrinsic consideration: "Because being thought of as a Latino writer was necessary to affirm the verisimilitude of the book and to promote sales of the book as 'real slice-of-life' work about Hispanic East Los Angeles." He suggests, moreover, that James himself did not trust the novel to stand on its own merit, and I suspect that he is at least partly correct, disclaimers to the contrary notwithstanding.

But are we more interested in the author or the work? *Famous All Over Town* is a good novel, not as strong as the short story that spawned it, but well above average. What Dan James is depends upon who you ask; he has advocates as well as detractors in the Mexican-American community. In any case, none of us exercises control over James, or any other writer, but we can determine our own response to fiction. If we read a novel ingeniously as a social document, then *who* wrote it takes on great importance—if only because some choose to believe that artists mirror *lumpen* experience rather than their own perceptual filters. Reading a novel as a work of art emphasizes the book itself and what it catalyzes in the reader. This is an approach that commentators such as Jonah Raskin, William McPherson and Joseph Kraft commended after "the Santiago hoax" was exposed. Of course, these two modes of apprehension are by no means mutually exclusive. More than a few of my acquaintances decry Dan James' deception while they still admire his book, albeit with variously altered perspectives.

But a larger issue is raised by all this, one that once haunted all western American literature: who can write what, or at least who should? Finally, most attacks on Santiago/ James hinge on the issue of authenticity. Again, it is Ortego y Gasca who offers the most interesting comment: "We can praise the verisimilitude in Seltzer's stories and the verisimilitude in James' novel. But that is not the same as authenticity." True enough. But there are many authentic Chicanos and authentic Anglos and authentic what-have-you's writing authentically lousy fiction. Taken to its extreme—and this has already been suggested by some critics—no male should write about female characters, for instance, and vice versa. Authors should forget research and dampen imagination, or label everything they write as "fantasy" unless it is strictly autobiographical. In reality, it must be acknowledged that critics— both Chicano and non-Chicano—became concerned with the authenticity of James' work only after his actual identity was disclosed. The same is true of Seltzer.

Katharine Newman, who founded MELUS (The Society for the Study of Multi-Ethnic Literature of the United States), adds a challenging dimension when she writes: "After fifteen years of fighting against the sloppy (and bigoted) argument that it is the 'literary worth' that matters, not the depiction of 'ethnic culture,' I feel the danger in Santiago/James' deception." Literary worth matters if we're talking about literature. Period. But it is not all that matters.

This country's racist history has led to cultural ignorance and willingness to accept stereotypes. As a result, readers tend to extrapolate generalities about ethnic groups from what they read, including fiction, as any teacher of ethnic literature can attest. So if a Dan James or a Chester Seltzer produces an inaccurate picture of his feigned culture, he can inadvertently distort the only perception of that people a reader may have: clearly dangerous business.

While I strongly disagree with Newman's apparent disdain for "literary worth," I do empathize with her concern that slickly written fiction of the *Hanta Yo* or *Confessions of Nat Turner* variety not be confused with genuine ethnic expression. Still, the mere fact that a nonmember of a given group writes about it does not necessarily invalidate that work: research is a legitimate tool of an author. *All other things being equal,* though, it is safe to assume that a gifted Chicano will write better novels of Chicano life than will a gifted Anglo. That all other things are not consistently equal complicates matters.

Hovering around theoretical discussions is the concrete recognition that many readers *will* study a work of the imagination as a social tract; the continuing debate over the "reality" of *The Grapes of Wrath*, for example, usually ignores the fact that Steinbeck's novel is true to the human spirit rather than to California history. There are delicate balances to be recognized here because mere literary skill does not make one a spokesperson for an ethnic group any more than does work that is unskilled though authentic. By the same token, there is no reason that an author like Steinbeck may not employ definably ethnic characters or settings to achieve universality. Some readers will misunderstand *Tortilla Flat* or the *The Grapes of Wrath*, but is that reason to condemn the books? It simply isn't that easy, although there have been times in the not-too-distant past when many of us acted as though it were.

Moreover, authenticity is not the objective criterion it appears to be. For example, within "ethnic criticism" there exist arguments over degrees of authenticity: who, for example, is the *most* authentic Chicano? Richard Rodriquez and Richard Vasquez are presently out *(demasiado asimilacion)*, while Miguel Mendez and Ron Arias are in *(muy carnalismo)* among cognoscenti, possibly for good reason, but the point is that authenticity frequently boils down to subjective judgments.

No one—not Ortego y Gasca or Newman or me—is qualified to say who can or should write what. That is a decision each artist must make and it will be based upon talent and craft and industry. As a courtesy to readers, however, American authors should use their own names or nondeceptive variations thereof, if only to avoid reinforcing traditions of bigotry and exploitation. In the last analysis, it is the deception implicit in Seltzer's and James' uses of *noms de plume*—no matter how innocent their intentions—that raises the issue of authenticity. But their cases exemplify more than errors in individual judgments: they also indict America's crass publishing industry and its passion to gorge on the commercial value of *anything*, including a Hispanic name; they indict as well over-compensatory critics who laud marginal writers and writing, creating a route to easy praise.

Finally, it is correct that artistic merit not authenticity remain the central criterion in judging a work's importance, since it is precisely the "literary worth" of Hinojosa's *Estampas Del Valle*, Rivera's *y no lo trago la tierra*, and Anaya's *Bless Me Ultima* that marks them as significant literature; their authenticity is a terrific bonus, but if they weren't written magically and skillfully, it would be of little consequence.

Who can write what? Anyone can write anything but, given this country's discriminatory past, integrity may be as important as talent when even implicit assertions of ethnic authenticity are present.

GROWING UP AT BABE'S [1985]

Our last meeting seems, in retrospect, fated. I had not been home for a long while and had not visited the gym for a couple of years, yet that day I drove to Bakersfield determined to catch a workout and banter with one of my few real friends, Babe Cantieny. I had just completed my first year of college teaching and was writing my first book, so I was full of my career; ties to my hometown had not lately loomed large on my mind, but I was determined to correct that.

When I didn't find Babe in the gym, I wandered downtown window shopping until, unexpectedly, I spied him near the California Theater, or him in miniature, for he had shrunken. He was still the well-proportioned, muscular man I had known, but he looked more like a finely conditioned lightweight boxer than a body builder. When I commented on his altered physiognomy, he gave me a crooked smile and said he was dropping a little weight for definition, then we moved to other topics.

We spent most of that afternoon talking, and he uncharacteristically brought up a couple of old misunderstandings, a couple of rough edges in our relationship. Babe wanted, it was clear, to make certain that we had everything in order, but it didn't dawn on me that he might also be saying goodbye. Our conversation, while deep at times, was not morose; we found a good deal to laugh about: the time a greenhorn challenged Charlie Bear Ahrens to a strength contest; the shenanigans we'd observed in the decrepit hotel across the street; the traffic cop who'd finally figured out that I was recycling an old parking ticket on my windshield for nearly a month while I worked out upstairs unconcerned about feeding a meter. It was a good day, one of the best.

A few months later, my mother sent me the clipping from the *Bakersfield Californian* that told me Marion "Babe" Cantieny, local businessman, was dead at 41. Then I understood what had occurred on our last afternoon together. Then, too, I finally admitted how important that short, quiet man had been in my life. I sat for a long time alone on my sun porch, too old to weep, reading and rereading the clipping: remembering, remembering . . .

I had begun lifting weights at Babe's Gym in June of 1954, seven years after Cantieny had opened it near the corner of 20th and Eye Streets. I was a 140-lb. weakling who had not made the football team at Garces High School the previous season. A chum named Charles Tripp convinced me to train there, even though in those days weight lifting was considered hazardous; there were ominous rumors that a few workouts might leave you "muscle bound," unable to tie your own shoes. Still, a friend at Garces, John Renfree, had used weights to go from a pudgy sub to an all-league tackle, and he seemed to tie his shoes with ease.

This was the dawn of the weight-training revolution that has so altered competitive sports. In fact, every athlete I knew in Bakersfield who lifted weights during that period did so at Babe's; he was without question a pioneer in introducing the technique to the area's athletes, especially football players.

Babe, himself, seemed quietly intimidating that first day when Tripp introduced us. All I could see were his bulging biceps as he sat behind his small desk in the cubbyhole he then employed as an office. He was all business as he made out a routine for me and walked me through it. Over that summer he twice altered my schedule of exercises to insure full range of motion and development. I noticed that he was always watching to make certain that all of us did our exercises properly and that no one hurt himself. He was quick to correct flawed techniques, demonstrating them until you grasped the proper method.

Babe had a few close friends among his clientele, chums with whom I'd hear him open up, laugh and romp a bit, but basically he was private without being cold. I realized then that he was far different, far deeper than the brooding adolescents with whom inexperience had at first led me to identify him. His silence was not a threat because he did not need to threaten.

There were rules of conduct at Babe's Gym and they were not breached, not twice anyway. Even in those days when young bucks all thought they had to be fighters, I never saw an argument get out of hand among the youthful studs pumping themselves up. It was clear that nonsense wouldn't be tolerated. Once—this would be in 1957—two large Bakersfield College football players began wrestling among the weights. Babe said only, "Hey!" and they froze. Later, I walked into the dressing room while the two, each appearing twice Babe's size, were gazing at the floor and the proprietor was softly saying something like, "If you can't respect other people's rights, don't come back." They came back but never disrupted workouts again.

The atmosphere at the gym was convivial; as Mike Janzen recently observed, it was like one big family. Babe's Gym remains for me, over thirty years after I first entered it and nearly twenty-five since I've been an active member, my club, the only one I ever belonged to in my hometown, the only one I ever needed. It featured a rugged but not raw male comradery, with joshing and kidding the principal forms of communication. Taking yourself too seriously was not tolerated, although genuine problems were dealt with compassionately.

I especially recall how the older guys shaped up the younger. Once, in my loudmouth youth, I referred to a middle-aged musician's spouse as his "old lady," a cute term that wowed my pals. He turned to me and asked, "Do you mean my *wife*?" I was thirty years younger and twenty pounds heavier than him, but I got the message. "Yes sir," I replied; "Sorry." Doing the correct thing, I learned, was not the same as backing down, and I don't think I've called any woman that again. Mutual respect required, most of all, that it *be* mutual. From such lessons is maturity built. They were taught that way because mutual respect and acceptance were the rule, not the exception—you had to *prove* yourself a jerk in order to be rejected, possibly ejected—which was a reflection of Babe's

LIBRARY ST. MARY'S COLLEGE

own personality. If a guy couldn't be comfortable at the gym, he probably couldn't be comfortable.

About 1958, Babe fell on hard times. Big chains of workout salons (we called them "saloons") were opening in town, with high-pressure salesmen pushing "life memberships" which promised profit for the gyms in the guise of bargains for prospective members. The salons featured steam baths and plush carpets and newfangled exercise machines. Babe's customers were dazzled by the dramatically lower rates such joints advertised, and some began drifting away. Moreover, new customers became as rare as saints. Not knowing what else to do, Babe opened a second gym on Baker Street and tried to compete with the chains, even selling life memberships, something that would haunt him for the remainder of his days.

I was inducted into the army that year. When I returned home on leave, Babe had lost his gyms and, to a degree, his self-respect. It was a painful time, because his family life had fallen apart too. But he didn't leave town or hide; he was in fact fighting back, determined to reopen the gym and to try to make good on the memberships that had been forfeited when his business had gone belly-up. "Your reputation is really all you've got," he told me, "and when something like this happens, it seems like everything turns bad, but you can't give up, you've got to work your way back." He did.

I had listened then as later because, without being heavy-handed, Babe had become an advisor to me, and his willingness to acknowledge his own frailties and problems made his counsel all the more valuable. He was the first adult who had ever really confided in me. When I was considering marrying a girl my friends advised against—"It'll never last . . ."—I talked to Babe, who also knew her. He told me about his own failed marriage, and suggested that many of the conventional, romanticized generalizations about marriage were bunk. "Marry someone you can get along with, that's what's most important. You can have the hots for anyone, but be sure you get along. Then put away the past—everyone's got one—and start from scratch. You two will be okay. I think it will work." I married her and, nearly twenty-five years later, remain grateful that I did.

In one limited area, the student became teacher. Babe, like most white men of his generation, harbored misgivings about nonwhites. This is not to say that he was a racist—he certainly was not—but he had little experience with nonwhites and, like many in those unenlightened times, accepted certain stereotypes. In any case, I was, as he once called me, "the resident liberal." We talked often and not very expertly, I'm afraid, about race and ethnicity. Some others in the gym hinted that they'd resent having to work out with nonwhites. When push came to shove and a black East High football player climbed the twenty-eight steps to the gym, Babe signed him up, gave him his routine and, without saying a word, let it be known that he would, like the rest of us, be given the benefit of the doubt.

That occurred, of course, well before the Civil Rights Movement grasped the nation and rattled Kern County, so Babe's act, however insignificant it may seem today, was a long way from business-as-usual then. We talked about that, Babe and I, during our final afternoon together and, while he had by no means joined the NAACP, he acknowledged that I had been correct when I'd urged him to judge each nonwhite as he would each white, individually. I'm glad that I was able to return some small slip of wisdom.

During my initial summer of training at Babe's Gym, once I had realized that Babe was friendly in his quiet way, I'd begun working out during off-hours when there were few others present, and that had led to conversations with him, perfunctory and superficial at first, then deeper and more candid. Eventually I admitted feeling that I had let my father down by not sticking with football the previous year, and he sensed correctly that my too-frequent bravado hid an aching insecurity. He advised me gently and earnestly, then one day asked if I wanted to play baseball. With special friends, when the gym was otherwise empty, he'd pitch a cork—the missile spinning in odd and unpredictable directions—while a batter flailed futilely with a narrow stick. It was a laughing time but, more than that, it was a symbol of acceptance. And if Babe could accept me, I could accept myself.

I played football for Garces the following season, even made a contribution; I went on to play a bit in college and in the service, my lean frame bulked up to a massive 165 pounds. I continued lifting at Babe's—except for those years away in the army—until I departed for good in 1961. I still lift three days a week using the routines Babe taught me, at home now with my own kids, none of whom, alas, ever was lucky enough to know Babe. And I still weigh 165; while I'm wearing my hair thinner and my wrinkles deeper, I continue to wear the same size clothing. Best of all, I can still tie my shoes. The habit of fitness came early, and it came from Babe's Gym.

I write this remembrance on Babe's old wall desk, the very one at which he noted in his precise hand my routine that summer afternoon 1954. He gave me the desk when I went away to college and it has seen me through three degrees. Moreover, all of my books, all of my stories, all of my articles— my entire career, really—have been written on it. Like my past and my town and my friends, with all their imperfections, it will do. I don't expect ever to replace it.

BREAKING THE MIGRANT CYCLE   [1977]

Nearly half of Nuevo Chupicuaro's 5,000 inhabitants have trekked north again this year to work around King City in the heart of California's Salinas Valley. Many of Nuevo Chupicuaro's other residents have also traveled to the Golden State where they too are providing experienced field labor during peak seasons for American farmers, especially in the San Joaquin Valley southeast of King City. In fact, very few citizens remain in this small Mexican town in the state of Guanajuato, other than those too young or too old to endure the journey and the tough, if rewarding toil that has become the village's economic base.

From the points of view of both American growers and Mexican laborers, the migration is successful. The former depend on a mobile labor force, while the latter are able to significantly improve their standards of living. "They are well paid for their work and nearly all own their own homes in Nuevo Chupicuaro," recently reported the *Rustler*, a newspaper published in this Salinas Valley town. "We are very content to work here," Robert Garcia told Jeanie Abel, a local journalist.

The paper's feature on satisfied migrant laborers was published at a fortuitous—perhaps too fortuitous—time, because King City is the center of a continuing controversy over farm laborers who want to stop migrating and settle here. If many locals claim it is a contrived fuss, drummed up by the ubiquitous and cunning media, and those fabled outside agitators with nothing better to do than stir up trouble in small towns, the dispute nonetheless appears to have roots in this state's complex history of farm labor.

In King City this year a group of migrants, not Mexicans but Americans of Mexican descent, uttered the classic "Basta!" ("Enough!") and refused to continue their nomadic existence.

47

In effect, they declined to play by rules that have governed California agriculture since the 1870s.

As migrants, they had accepted a pattern established during the decade following the Civil War when California growers employed Chinese laborers—the backbone of much of this state's development—to convert vast wheatlands into more profitable fruit and vegetable farms. During the hundred plus years that have followed, Japanese, Southern Europeans, East Indians, Mexicans, Filipinos, Blacks, Okies, and now Mexicans, once again have provided the bulk of the labor force necessary to sustain what Carey McWilliams aptly labeled "factories in the fields," the large corporate farms that characterize California agriculture.

Most groups have willingly accepted the advantages and limitations of migrant farm work only during their early, desperate years in California, moving as soon as possible into more stable jobs and the economic mainstream. But in Mexicans and Mexican-Americans some growers have come to believe they have a permanent labor supply, a never-ending stream of people so poor that farm labor is always a step up. The border is close and porous, and a renewable first-generation of migrants is ever at hand.

The Golden State's agricultural industry has been built upon four pillars: good climate, rich soil, abundant water, and cheap labor. Disturb any one of them and the entire structure is threatened, as well as the huge, complementary economic and social web woven around it in the past century. Indeed, many farmers have come to believe that all four pillars are their due, so their usual kindness can evaporate suddenly when workers don't cooperate.

The confrontation in King City reveals forces at the core of rural California's economic and social life. Last March 26, ten families were evicted from a local farm labor camp, some four months after they were first ordered to leave. Four of the families built plywood and cardboard cabins next to the fence separating them from the county-operated housing project, which is by law open only 180 days a year in order to house migrants.

The "squatters," as they are called here, dramatically illustrate both the complexity of agricultural labor relations in the late twentieth century, and the paradox of poor who are willing to play by the rules as they understand them in order to claw their way into the much-maligned middle class, for these are hard-working people, most of whom have found steady jobs in the area. In that, they are also following a common California pattern: one generation struggling with menial agricultural labor while the next takes advantage of the educational system to break the cycle of poverty; this is the real and enduring promise of the Golden State. To do that at all well, however, it is necessary to establish something like a permanent residence so children can settle into schools. Then what's the fuss, since these are not welfare sponges but folks who have contributed to the society and hope to continue doing just that? Taken at face value, this is a much-heat little-light controversy with outrage the order of the day on all sides. Looked at more closely, it is a classic test of whether we truly believe the tenets of our own national credo.

Racism was an immediate charge by concerned Chicanos. Hector de la Rosa, a community worker for California Rural Legal Assistance, explained: "Our problem is, the way I see it, that there is a lot of discrimination in towns like King City. . . . They [Anglo residents] are concerned that some day Chicanos will outnumber them. So they try to keep them out."

Such charges were countered by a more recent, increasingly popular abstraction, "welfarism." In an editorial, the *Rustler* claimed that "the real reason behind the families' demonstration appears to be that they want to be provided with cheap housing and to hell with everyone else."

In any case, King City already boasts a substantial Chicano population. More than 40 of 107 Little League baseball players have Spanish surnames, as do 4 of 8 managers. It is also a town where social clubs reflect much less integration, and there are no Chicanos holding elected offices. Nonetheless, many Anglo and Chicano residents consider relations good. Intermarriages are not uncommon. More than a few residents of Mexican extraction admit they are embarrassed by the squatters. Class, not race or nationality, seems to be the core problem for them.

Not everyone in the Mexican-American community shares such views, however. Victor Manuel Navarro, one of the men evicted from the labor camp, told *San Francisco Examiner* reporter Raul Ramirez, "They don't want us in King City. If we get established here, who knows, maybe we'll vote and they'll lose their power. Now it's only the rich people who run the city. They don't want us participating, even if our work is what gives them the money to have the power." In fact, Navarro's assessment seems wisest of all for he has summed up California agriculture, its structure and its core dilemma: manual labor remains the base of the economic pyramid, and power—the pyramid's pinnacle—is the ultimate plum.

That brown people may one day recapture this region they once tenuously held is a fear spoken in hushed tones at lodge meetings and private parties: *We need them to work our fields, but what if. . . ? And, my God, bilingual education makes it that much easier for them to become voters. And cheap housing makes it that much easier for them to become voters. And now some are dating our kids. Why can't they just work then go back to Mexico?*

Slavery is no longer legal, but a plantation mentality and the belief that constant peonage is necessary, even good in a peculiar way, have by no means departed. The 180-day limit on housing for migrants is an attempt to guarantee the existence of a continued mobile labor force for growers, the serf-class necessary if business is to continue as usual.

Local newspapers, as well as television stations in Salinas and San Jose, had covered the growing dispute, but it was not until Ramirez's front-page story in the *Examiner* that widespread attention—including support for the four families from such diverse politicians as Senators S.I. Hayakawa and Edward Kennedy, and California's Lieutenant Governor, Mervyn Dymally—riveted on King City. Ramirez left no doubt about his own sympathies as he told how the families pursued the

American Dream: a steady job, a home, and most profoundly, a decent education for their children so that they, at least, might finally escape continued peonage.

Housing—especially low-cost housing—is an enduring problem in the area. The *Rustler* was quick to introduce the shortage of homes in an impassioned editorial response to the Ramirez article, explaining why the city was not responsible. State law controls the camp, it was claimed, but Lionel Alvarado, chief of migrant services, says the state is powerless. Bruce Moore, county housing authority director, explains, "There is no legal way that the . . . housing can be unlocked until the voters of King City say yes."

Still the *Rustler* insisted that "King City has nothing to say in governing the camp," and based upon that claim, the editorial ostensibly clarified matters: "At issue here is an attempt through a demonstration to force a change in state law; to provide cheap housing to those who cannot or do not wish to pay regular housing costs in this area."

Ignored in the editorial was the fact that local voters negated a referendum that would have allowed the development of fifty units of low-rent residences by the housing authority. The *Salinas Californian* noted that "the root problem . . . reflects King City's greater willingness to meet the needs of the moving migrant than the low-income Mexican American." True enough, so the important question is why the essentially decent and friendly people of King City feel as they do. History provides at least part of the answer.

Contrary to popular belief, California growers did not employ large numbers of Mexican field laborers until the 1920s. This fact is a reflection of population patterns; as David Lavender explains, "In 1900 there had been only 8,000 Mexicans in California—an erstwhile Mexican province! But in 1920 there were 121,000 and ten years later 368,000." At least 150,000 Mexicans followed the crops during the twenties. It seemed a grower's dream: an endless supply of migrants who were hard workers, and it was generally agreed that they were somehow "suited" for field labor, a racial stereotype still popular in rural California, where more than a few whites also seem unable—possibly just unwilling—to distinguish between Chicanos and migrants from Mexico, calling both "Mexicans," with the strong connotation of "foreigner," more than a little ironic since so many Anglos are themselves recent migrants from the Midwest and Southwest.

By the time the Great Depression hit California, a more ominous characteristic had surfaced among the migrant laborers: left-wing labor unions from Mexico provided leadership when, in 1930-31, Mexican and Filipino workers—the same ethnic combination that would eventually form the United Farm Workers a quarter-century later—struck various growers. The specter of a union, any union, terrified agricultural interests, and long-held assumptions concerning Latin docility were quickly rejected.

In 1930, urban relief officials had initiated a voluntary repatriation program for Mexicans. After the strikes, some old timers claim today, the program both accelerated and became less voluntary. In any case, by 1937 an estimated 150,000 people had been shipped to Mexico, including some American citizens.

The next big influx of Mexican laborers occurred during the Korean War with the passage of Public Law 78, which allowed growers throughout the Southwest to import workers from south of the border. In 1964, Congress ended the program, despite grower protests, and the stage was set for the organization of farm labor in California.

There were nearly 200,000 nonimported casual farm laborers in the state at the time, certainly an ample base. Moreover, charismatic leaders had arisen: Larry Itliong of the largely Filipino-American Agricultural Workers Organizing Committee and Cesar Chavez of the mostly Mexican-American National Farm Workers Association. Both men were determined not to allow growers the traditional ploy of pitting one ethnic group against another, so the two bodies amalgamated into the United Farm Workers Organizing Committee, and a new era dawned in California agriculture.

Unionization has been a major factor in slowing the stream of migrants for, as De La Rosa points out, "The union tends to stabilize the work force." Locally, the UFW has strongly supported the squatters. Two of the men living outside the King City camp, Navarro and Vicente Robles, are union members, a fact that has gained them scant support locally because the union is still viewed with scorn. King City wasn't the only hot spot in rural California. At Hollister in nearby San Benito County, the board of supervisors unanimously turned down a bid by state officials to allocate some $365,000 for improvements such as indoor toilets at another of the twenty-five camps in the state, all limited to 180 days of occupancy a year. Leonard Alvarado reported that the action was in all likelihood a prelude to closing the facility, a step that could force many migrants back toward the ditchbank settlements of the brutal past.

San Benito County officials cited the overloading of the local sewage-treatment plant as the reason for their decision, plus the inconvenience posed by over 100 migrant children suddenly enrolling in a nearby country school that usually served only 20 pupils. Frank Sabbatini, chairman of the board of supervisors, revealed the most important reason for the rejection when he explained: "The big concern is that if improvements are allowed to be put in, the camp might become a permanent housing project."

Like King City, San Benito County suffers from a serious shortage of low-cost housing. Ten days after their controversial decision, the San Benito supervisors reversed themselves after state officials agreed to not only refurbish the camp, but to help deal with sewage and school overcrowding problems as well. Observed California's assistant secretary of health and welfare: "That was real government in action: the board responding to the will of the people."

The controversy also reveals an emerging reality in California's life, an ironic hidden agenda, given the state's history: many whites feel political control gradually but certainly slipping away, Mexicans winning back what they lost in the Treaty of Guadalupe Hidalgo. The irony is doubled, however, when one realizes that the so-called Mexicans who are gaining prominence in state affairs—no matter how loyal they are to traditional Latin values—are really Californians, the products of a complex, rich society that bends everyone toward what Kevin Starr has called "The California Dream," an almost limitless sense of the possible.

About midway between Hollister and King City, an example of that dream is developing. A group of migrant families, all of Mexican extraction, have scored a hard-earned victory over bureaucratic inflexibility. Four years ago, several farm laborers banded together to purchase a crumbling bracero camp. They hoped to create what they called the San Jerardo Community, a worker-owned farm labor camp. Last month, the first two of sixty projected units were completed, up to county codes and ready for occupancy, but they will remain empty a while longer; "We all agreed that until the last one is built they should remain unused," explained Juan Aleman. Since owners are doing most of their own work, it may take considerably more time but, says Aleman, "Now we know it can be done."

One problem the San Jerardo Community had faced was a lawsuit by fifteen property owners challenging the permit that had allowed housing to be constructed in the agricultural area. None of the plaintiffs had sued when the camp housed braceros or other migrant laborers.

Back in King City, matters were finally coming to a head. Stung by widespread criticism, city authorities posted the migrants' hovels with notices declaring them structurally unsafe, a first step in removing them. Meanwhile, the squatters were unsuccessful in seeking alternative housing. A week later—ironically, on the same day some of the erstwhile migrants traveled to Sacramento to appeal for help—city workers dismantled the shacks.

By then, however, the state had moved in its own heavy artillery. Secretary of health and welfare Mario Obledo intervened, offering the families housing at nearby Camp Roberts, a national guard base busy only during summers. He also personally asked county housing director Bruce Moore to reopen the camp early and to allow the families to stay there.

Like other problems in California agriculture, the King City situation remains unresolved. One obvious compromise would be for local authorities to allow the squatters to reside in camp year-round if family members, in turn, continue to provide seasonal farm labor. It's a compromise with which the evicted families have no trouble, since they intend to supplement their steady income with farm labor when the season arrives.

Also, projects like the San Jerardo Community should be encouraged, with public assistance loans made available, since such efforts really do assist the public, something of a rarity. Any long-term solution, of course, must involve more low-cost housing so that poor families, too, might reasonably hope to share America's promise.

King City and the rural towns around it are not hotbeds of racism or nativism, but the good, hard-working citizens of the region too often use the products of poverty and denied opportunity to justify continued poverty and denial of opportunity, an insidious trap. Moreover, many choose to believe that Mexicans and Chicanos are different—somehow uniquely suited for field labor—so they thoughtlessly impose difficult conditions on them.

But the situation is even more complicated because many local farmers can point to similar hardships in their own lives or those of family members, and they can honestly say they would become migrant laborers if necessary for survival. They would do so, however, only as one step toward stable lives, not as career transients whose children would be career transients. It is in their willingness to believe that others do not similarly aspire for better lives that they manifest symptoms of a continuing California social disease.

OILDALE [1987]

To gaze deep within myself, I walk the streets of Oildale. On December 23, 1985, a frigid tule fog obscuring all but the nearest yards and houses, I wander up McCord Street—no sidewalks here, but many trailer parks in an area where once Dust-Bowl migrants built hovels—and I notice two banty roosters scratching and jerking on a patch of brown bermuda grass, eyeing one another but ignoring, as nearly as I can tell, two wild doves feeding with them. I stop and for a few moments stand motionless, watching while my breath bursts white, then one dove flies with a muffled whir and the other poses warily. Both roosters pause, fighters awaiting the bell.

With a hollow warble, the second dove climbs swiftly into the gray surrounding us, leaving me on the sandy border between lawn and street. I notice then two pickups parked on the far border of the bermuda, one ancient and huge, the other new, small and crowned with four yellow fog lights. On the older vehicle's blotched surface someone has painted "Trust Jesus." A bumper sticker on the new one says, "If you love something, set it free. If it returns, it is yours. If it doesn't, hunt it down and kill it." The smaller pickup is metallic red, as are the roosters.

The neighborhood through which I wander is called Riverview because before a dam was constructed in the mountains east of town, you could view the Kern River flowing through your kitchen during wet winters. It was once considered the least prosperous section in this unaffluent and unincorporated community. Today, although new housing developments sprout on Oildale's outskirts, many of the same unpainted shanties I used to see here as a kid in the 1940s remain erect and apparently unchanged—like tribal elders, reminders of our collective past. Two or three rickety lawn chairs—poor people's air conditioners—sit in front of many such residences, as do cars or trucks whose grandeur often contrasts sharply with the setting.

Such older houses are now bracketed by ubiquitous trailer parks and what realtors like to call upgraded houses. The former feature everything from modern mobile homes complete with metallic awnings and metallic porches, to geriatric travel trailers, faded and frayed. Most of the upgraded houses are carefully painted and their yards may be tended by dark-skinned men from other communities; moreover, there seem to be more and more signs announcing security systems, indicating perhaps a seige mentality, the long shadow of hard times past.

Now contiguous with Bakersfield, Oildale grew north of the larger town during the early years of this century. Lawrence Clark Powell worked in the area in the early 1920s and even then, he tells me, "We learned to leave the Oildale guys alone, thank you." It was an enclave of oil-company camps, attracting a disproportionate number of males who did hard, physical labor, and pursued rough, masculine diversions. Except that agriculture and not petroleum was the principal lure, this was also the pattern for much of the San Joaquin Valley, where waves of migrants have been attracted since the 1870s not by gold nuggets or movie careers but by the availability of what can only be called toil: Chinese, Japanese, East Indians, Mexicans, Filipinos, Blacks, plus many varieties of Whites.

Despite their resulting heterogeneity, most agricultural towns have by no means been racially integrated but have at least hosted residents of varied colors, whereas the oil industry, unofficially but actually, did not welcome nonwhites. So towns like Taft, Coalinga and Oildale developed racist reputations. In my youth there was even said to have been a sign— which no one ever saw but everyone talked about—on the outskirts of town: "Nigger, don't let the sun set on you here."

In any case, my hometown's renown as a rough section intensified following the so-called Dust-Bowl migration of the 1930s when large numbers of Southwesterners settled here.

This is Merle Haggard's home town; Buck Owens' Enterprises is a major local business. Today, fifty years after that migration began in earnest, and now boasting its own hospital, its own high school, its own civic organizations, Oildale is nonetheless spoken of by local liberals as a redneck enclave.

A close friend of mine—a Bakersfield boy who under-stands well what my hometown *means* locally—mentioned the other night that his therapist had suggested that Oildale is a crucible for fascism, which might simply mean that people here voted for Ronald Reagan, hyperbole being what it is. But my friend guessed that the three R's—racism and rowdiness and the right to bear arms—were troubling her, so he rattled the therapist's cage, telling her about the night a group of us, all high school pals, had driven to my house from Bakersfield. In our exaggerated sense of adventure, we had suggested that the one black among us duck as we entered Oildale—he'd laughingly complied—then we had dashed from the car into my place where we'd spent the night.

While our dramatics were unnecessary, they symbolize an aspect of Oildale's lingering reputation among those who do not live here: it is said to be an environment unconducive to notions as diverse as affirmative action, gun control, cigarette warnings, and seat belts. More to the point, Oildale has been to Bakersfield as Bakersfield has been to California, a scapegoat; "You're from *Oildale?*" I've heard at genteel parties, tone saying it all.

It is also what thin-wristed experts like to call a working-class area, and it remains predominantly white. Because so many of Oildale's citizens over the years have been fair-skinned Southwesterners, lovers of country music and the self-serving version of patriotism it posits, the community has been assigned a gothic Southern stereotype. This has been aided by the more important fact that many white migrants were poorly educated, products of generations of yeomanry, so they had to compete with nonwhites for jobs on nearby farms or work in the now-integrated oilfields. More than a little local pontification on matters racial has been in fact an expression of economic fear.

Racism, as well as other narrowness, hangs on most desperately among the desperate, but in this state it cannot be easily separated from issues of social class, for the latter, usually unspoken but as real and as certain as the surging of sex, often triggers racist regression. Here in California some nonwhites—the number need not be large, only visible—have been able to take advantage of the state's educational system to escape chronic destitution and assumed inferiority. While the society as a whole benefits from such a development, to whites stranded on that same desperate level, the underclass, even the slightest gain for nonwhites is clear evidence that something is wrong with America: *This is white country but a damn Mescan's bossin' me. Shee-it!* This is one reason why racist organizations tend to contain so many marginal members rather than men and women of accomplishment; the former are the threatened ones.

In the court of $225-a-month houses across the street from my folks' place, I see fair-skinned young men with long unkempt hair, bearded, disheveled, angry after three beers at a world that does not offer them well-paid jobs or much prestige, but does provide drug dealers to rip them off and does provide candy-bar and soda-pop lunches. They carry homemade tattoos on their knuckles, and their shoulders are splendid with murals of nude women on horses, but few high school diplomas grace their mantels: school sucks, man. If asked, they will often reveal that they are about to tell someone off or to kick someone's ass.

Christmas Eve, 1984, I walked out of my mother and father's small house and heard howls and screams from the courts: one young man was beating another in the street while two women shrieked and a third man yelled encouragement. The puncher was shouting over and over at the punchee something like "Take my fuckin' money!" It was not a new scene to me, but that night it struck me: those cries should have echoed through the halls of Congress, or through that therapist's office, because they were battling each other in lieu of opponents they could neither see nor understand. And I, raised on this street, having seen my father fight here and having bled

LIBRARY ST. MARY'S COLLEGE

59

here myself, fresh from a comfortable Christmas celebration with my family, I knew exactly what was going on, and was swept by imprecise guilt along with enormous gratitude for my own good fortune. But I did not allow myself to say, "There but for the grace of God go I," for I did indeed go there, or at least some part of me did. A moment later, a sheriff's cruiser pulled up and I returned to the warmth of family within my parents' house, reminded as my hometown frequently reminds me of the proximity and the possibility of poverty, and of its consequences.

Not only young men dwell in those $225-a-month units. My own grandmother lived in one—$50 a month then—and those small houses have long been refuges for the impecunious old. Many young women reside there too, more all the time it seems, often single mothers, also poorly educated and often tattooed—a small butterfly on a shoulder, a rose on one breast. In their too-young, too-fleeting primes they may combine bad teeth with bodies that make men gnaw chrome, but their boyfriends gnaw something else and soon babies ride on each hip; with them come food stamps, hours watching daytime television and, usually, revolving males who cannot support themselves, let alone families; and with them may come the unfocused outrage that accompanies an erosion of hope.

As is true of people floundering at the bottom, these young and old, women and men, tend not to see over the rim to reality, so they remain frustrated by and angry at a world that offers them only blue-light specials. And when things go wrong, as they so persistently do, someone must be blamed: mother dies and the damned doctors are responsible; the car doesn't run and the dirty Japs are guilty; I don't get the job because that other bastard has suck. Niggers cause this, and Jews, and slopes, but mostly niggers because blaming blacks has long been an acceptable way for lower-class whites to vent general grievances. Anyway, Rambo or Jimmy Swaggert or the Klan will save us—white men banded together. And no niggers better move into Oildale because this is white people's territory; at least we're better than niggers. It is an irrational, probably unavoidable stance, one held with the desperate, uncritical grip of divine revelation: it *must* be true.

My own parents, for reasons I've never fully understood—his better education, probably, and her Latin attitudes—but for which I remain constantly grateful, did not indulge in such delusion. Instead, they taught me to accept people as individuals; my dad's dictum, for example, was "Is he a good guy?" not "Is he colored?" Thus Quincy Williams and Freddie Dominguez and John Takeuchi slept and ate at our house, just as did Raymie Meyer and Ernie Antongiovanni and Tommy Alexander. If my folks had only given me that I would have been well served.

Poverty and race and class churn a bitter stew: history dictates that a much larger proportion of blacks than whites inhabits the dungeon of unabating want, so race has been and remains an effective camouflage for our system's inability to reach many endemic poor. Because it is convenient to keep the hungry fighting one another, racism is frequently *part* of poverty, just as idealized egalitarianism is *part* of liberalism: default assumptions.

I must challenge my pal's therapist: Oildale is not a breeding ground for fascism, but poverty certainly is, poverty and ignorance and hopelessness so deep that education and government programs cannot deflect it. My hometown is a place where low-rent housing and the rumor of jobs for the unskilled has traditionally attracted whites on the bottom hoping to struggle toward the middle.

Those who do make that transition may carry lower-class fears and prejudices longer than is conscionable, but the real problem is that others never make it. In Oildale you cannot be unaware of this nation's class system because this is a cusp where hopelessness and hope, or at least the *hope* of hope, abut. When even that slimmest of threads frays, despair engulfs and violence erupts, in Oildale as elsewhere.

Therein lies the rub. Without this community and its unpretentious styles, many people would be utterly abandoned by a society that fears fascism or attacks socialism but dreads and distrusts losers most of all, would be ignored by an elite often willing to love the poor only as it imagines them, not as they are: hopeless as well as hopeful. Since the poor exist, they must exist somewhere, and Oildale predictably harbors a proportionate number of losers: *Who's got the dope, man?*

But the losers constitute a small if visible minority here. I stride past the Assembly of God on Wilson Street, and from within I hear voices raised to a God who can accept, and I hear people—some of them from the courts, grown broad-hipped and repentant—praying for me, their brother burdened by sins unknown to them, but burdened, surely burdened, because that is the human condition and with God's help it can be endured. In that congregation now as in the neighborhood, one might find a sprinkling of dark faces reflecting the slow erosion of stereotypes as well as the enduring truth that class profoundly influences the acceptance of nonwhites—too rich or too poor excluded. Unfortunately, the continued lack of blacks also illustrates the persistence of America's most heinous racist illusion.

What fearers of fascism forget is that most of Oildale is populated by folks who have established themselves in the middle class by dint of hard work, survivors whose daughters now aim for honor roll and university, whose sons play football and fight wars. Oildale's citizens pay their taxes, frequently resent welfare and shake their heads at punk rock, at "Fit 'n' Forty" medallions, at sprout sandwiches, but accept the churning present anyway. When I stroll through town, nearly everyone I meet says hello, often with a Southwestern drawl. Folks I've never seen before discuss the weather—"This *dern* fog . . ." —while waiting for traffic to pass. Their children have no drawls at all.

I notice other things on my visits home, little glimpses I no longer take for granted. On North Chester Avenue, aging men and women who struggled here from Oklahoma now drink coffee in a McDonald's that is identical with several in Tulsa. There seems to be an inordinate number of "Beware of Dog" signs, especially on those blocks populated by folks who have edged into the middle class. And on winter mornings if fog doesn't obscure the world, steam plumes rise from the hills north where, on the leases that lured so many here, leases where my father and I worked, heavy oil is liquified by the hot vapor then pumped to the surface.

It seems to me now that older women always boast hair care comparable to matrons in Palm Springs, their tresses freshly dyed, curled, piled and sprayed. Coiffures are taken seriously even if bodies are not. The other morning, at about 9 A.M., I passed a gal unlocking the front door of a beer bar, her hair deep red and elaborately swirled high above a leathery face imprinted "Texas, 1914." A cigarette dangled from her crimson lips when she smiled at me. I smiled back.

And there is an aggressive angle at which many men wear hats—billed caps, straw Stetsons, but no plaid snapbrims or berets—that advises you not to let your mouth overload your ass. Short sleeves may be rolled up, biceps bulging, and beer drinking after work seems sacramental, biceps bulging. Cars and guns are icons taken seriously, offering reasons for taking oneself seriously.

It is finally the mix of people hereabouts that most compels: friendly, plain-spoken, conservative, protestant in work ethic if not religion, scarred but not embittered by hard times, they constitute what I like to call a "front porch" society. In the days before air conditioners tamed the long, scorching summers, it was common for neighbors to gather on porches, drink iced tea, perhaps play cards or checkers, occasionally sing to the accompaniment of a guitar or banjo, but usually just talk. Many older folks still do these things, such gatherings livening balmy summer evenings, while kids clatter up and down sidewalks on skateboards now rather than skates.

Oildale is changing as the rest of California is, but its reputation is not altering apace. There is a sidewalk in front of my parents' place, built by the WPA in 1941, or so says the inscription on the corner. There is also a small parking strip there with a tree that has been so brutally trimmed that scar tissue knots it like tumors—a peculiar local style of arboreal coiffure that seems more ritual maiming than practical necessity. Below it, on summer mornings, runoff water from lawn irrigation settles in the gutter, a small pond, and every morning if I arise early I can sip coffee with my dad and watch doves drinking out there—an unchanging reality—dipping their fawn heads, bobbing their white-splashed tails. They rise with a whir when a truck bounces past on its way to the oilfields. Then the birds return, drink again and occasionally call—a haunting, hollow sound that says "Home."

ARNOLD R. ROJAS, VAQUERO   [1987]

An old wrangler named Ramon Dominguez first told me about Jefe Rojas. I was sixteen at the time, and Ramon was regaling his son Freddie and me as he often did with tales of nearly forgotten men, California's vaqueros. "There's this one guy I used to ride with that even wrote a book," he said, more wonder entering his voice than I ever heard when he spun yarns about magical figures such as *los chisos* or *la llorona*.

Ramon rarely avoided expanding a remark into a story when an audience was present, so he added, "My father said he seen this guy walking across a hay field years ago by San Emideo, no horse or nothing, just a bedroll, and he carried some books. The boss hired him. That guy he pulled the teeth of horses," added the aging hostler.

"He did *what*?" I asked. Ramon and his family lived then in an old, poor neighborhood of Bakersfield—once the state's cattle capital—a section near Union Cemetery populated largely by Hispanics, and this conversation occurred in the early 1950s when attentive youngsters could still listen to the recollections of men who had cowboyed on the ranges of Rancho Tejon, Miller and Lux, and the Kern County Land Company. Still, that was the first time I'd heard anyone mention pulling horses' teeth.

"He was horse dentist, that guy. Still is, I think."

I looked at Ramon's son, not certain I wasn't being roped. "No lie," Freddie nodded.

I listened that day to tales of the buckaroo who pulled horses' teeth, who read books, and who had now written one, but it wasn't until five years later—1958—that Freddie handed me a slim volume, *Lore of the California Vaqueros*, and I first read the work of Arnold R. Rojas, known locally as Jefe or Chief. In it I found a faithful sense of the stories told by old vaqueros, the voices of Dominguez and Urrea, Albitre and Garcia. It was like sitting under a tree on a long summer afternoon listening to *los viejos*.

What I didn't know was that *San Francisco Chronicle* book editor William Hogan had been so impressed with the same volume that he had referred to Rojas as "the vaqueros' Homer," and not without reason, for Jefe had written tale after fascinating tale, pulling them like a magician's endless chain of handkerchiefs.

For example, he recounted the experience of a buckaroo who tried to ride a bronco while wearing a pocket watch:

> The watch fastened to a buckskin thong dropped out of his vest pocket at the first jump and swung in an arch and hit the buckaroo in the nose. The next jump, the watch gave him a black eye and as long as the horse bucked, the watch swung. If the horse had not quit bucking, the watch "would have beat him to death," as the vaquero afterward said. He untied the buckskin thong and threw what was left of the watch as far away as he could.

He also recounted a meeting with Harry Gillem, a tough, black vaquero:

> Seeing that he was bandaged I asked him if he had been in an accident. He told me of having been set upon by three men. He had fought them until he had just about whipped all three, when one of them drew a knife and slashed him. Harry was cut badly and spent some time in a hospital. But he carried off the honors of war, however, because he had fought fair and when he was out of the hospital, two of the men with whom he had fought paid him $5.00 apiece to not fight with them again.

All of Rojas' books have been collections of sketches that, like much good folklore, straddle the boundary between history and fiction. A man of prodigious memory, he writes of incident after incident, character after character, no two exactly the same, revealing a world of proud, hard-working men.

"Professional vaqueros rode first for one company, then another," he writes. "A youngster, twelve to fourteen years of age, school not being compulsory, received a starting wage of $5.00 a month. After a year or two it was raised to $12.00 and it usually took five years of working experience to earn $25.00 a month. *Reatas* and hair ropes were furnished free to the vaqueros."

The language Rojas employs has merited critical comment. In the *Mexico City News*, Margaret Shedd observed that Rojas' use of Spanish featured *"espanol que no esta escrito"* ("Spanish that is not written"), California terms like *"chirrionero caballo pajarero"* ("a horse that shies at shadows") or *"agarrarse del sauce"* (literally, "take hold of the willow," meaning to grab the saddle horn when riding a bucking horse); it is the language of the folk not the professor, idiomatic and colorful, a product of the working men about whom he writes.

Now ninety years old, Jefe Rojas resides in Wasco, where he is writing his eighth book. He remains a living link to the great ranches of the last century. For a time he worked on Rancho Tejon, where he was hired by the legendary *mayordomo* J.J. Lopez, who ramrodded riders there from 1874 until 1939.

Rojas rode into a Tejon vaquero camp seeking work in the 1920s:

> I had sat down and was fixing something on my saddle when, looking up, I found watching me, an elderly man dressed in a pair of corduroy pants faded white from countless washings, a pair of World War I GI canvas leggings, a mohair coat affected by office workers of that period, shoes and an old hat. Surely, I thought, this couldn't be the renowned Don Jose Jesus Lopez.

It was. "I got the job," he continues, "and as time passed I found Don Jesus a man of many parts—shrewd, well educated, with a keen sense of humor."

Jefe was born in 1896 in Pasadena into a family that had migrated to California from the western Mexican states of Sonora and Sinaloa in the 1820s. His Indian ancestors were Yaquis and Mayos, while his Spanish progenitors were Sephardic Jews who migrated to the Americas to escape the Inquisition.

Following the death of his parents, the boy was placed in an orphanage in San Luis Obispo in 1902. He ran away when he was 12. "I wanted to come to the San Joaquin Valley and I did," he explains. He hoped to become a rider and the San Joaquin, along with the mountains that surround it, was cattle country.

He rode first for the V7 Ranch in San Luis, then on the vast San Emideo Ranch operated by the Kern County Land Company, and later on the Tejon. For the next quarter century, Rojas worked horses and cattle on the California range, knew its denizens, learned its legends.

In 1935 he purchased a stable in Bakersfield—"I called it the Bar-O because I borrowed everything"—and began serving as a dentist for horses. Both his location and his work kept him close to the men with whom he had toiled and many a warm afternoon was spent swapping yarns while leaning on a corral fence or hunkered next to a hay bale. He listened well.

From the start he had been different from most of his fellow vaqueros in one respect: he became self-educated, reading voraciously. As a teenager, he was staying at his uncle's cabin in Soledad Canyon near Acton when an aging neighbor— "He was starving out," Rojas explains—asked to be staked to some coffee, flour, beans, and sugar. The old man noticed that Rojas was reading an O. Henry "Heart of the West" tale in a magazine, so when he returned, he brought books—Dumas, Cervantes, Kipling, Irving—which he exchanged for the loan of food. That was the beginning of Rojas' literary training.

His reading was like frosting on a cake of practical knowledge, for he not only learned the technology of ranch work, as well as how to survive in a rough environment, but he also talked to men who claimed to have known the legendary bandit Joaquin Murrieta, to have eaten ostriches on the Rancho Tejon and to have ridden camels there, to have been singed by the Devil at San Emideo or to have confronted the fabled weeping woman, *la llorona*, in San Antonio.

Rojas became a writer following World War II when he was named chairman of a rodeo sponsored by the American Legion in Bakersfield. Jim Day, editor of the *Bakersfield Californian*, suggested that Jefe compose something that could be used as publicity for the event, so he wrote thumbnail sketches of several old vaqueros whom he planned to honor at the event. A few days later, the *cuentitos* appeared in Day's column, "Pipefuls." Thereafter, Jefe was an occasional contributor to the *Californian* and, in 1952, his work came to the attention of California historian Monsignor James Culleton, who eventually published three volumes of the ex-vaquero's tales at the Academy Library Guild in Fresno: *California Vaqueros* (1953), *Lore of the California Vaqueros* (1958), and *Last of the Vaqueros* (1960).

Visiting Jefe in Wasco over thirty years after first having been told about him, I ask if he remembers Ramon Dominguez. "Ramon, why sure. He was Frank's boy. He was a good old vaquero, Frank Dominguez, and he gave me a lot of material. Ramon worked as a teamster on the ranch."

Rojas is a man with strong opinions. When I inquire about the relationship of "old California families" and more recently migrated Mexicans, he responds: "When gringos entered the area and sought title to its riches, the only way to acquire the land was to marry a daughter of the landowner, and the gringos had already started a campaign of discrimination. They solved that problem by creating 'old Spanish families' and marrying into them. But those who had no lands left became Mexicans, doomed to work for cheap wages and to suffer discrimination.

"The gringos taught the paisanos to be ashamed of their race," he adds.

Has that changed much? I ask.

"Those of muddy complexions seem to suffer most, but not so much nowadays. The 'White Trade Only' signs are no longer posted, and one sees Mexican kids as news commentators, speaking faultless English, as managers of stores, banks, and other businesses." He smiles.

"When I was young I left Southern California because I refused to be a fruit picker. I came to the ranches but the only work a man of my race could get in those days was as a mule skinner or vaquero, both cheap labor."

The San Joaquin Valley—now conceded to be the richest agricultural area in the world—was different when Rojas entered it early in the century. He shakes his head. "Except for the lupins and poppies, which covered the valley in the spring, the country was semi-desert and the climate was horrible, with pea-soup fog in the winter, and 110 degrees in summer. No one ever thought it would be covered with orchards and vineyards as it is today."

Even then, he points out, the economic pattern of large land holdings characterized the region. "When I came here, three big companies owned most of this part of the valley, and the small farmer was poor indeed. Much of the land was left for cattle ranges."

Before I pose another question, he adds a postscript: "Today there are too many people."

Jefe remains a handsome man, lean and leathery with classic Western features. Standing on his porch and squinting into spring sunlight, he seems to encapsulate an aspect of California history. "I'm still working," he explains, "but it's harder. Sometimes I don't write for months. Most of the old timers who told me stories are dead, and it's getting harder to find material."

When *These Were the Vaqueros: The Collected Works of Arnold R. Rojas* was published in 1974, the old horseman placed his writing in perspective: "I started as a skinny kid, and the men I admired were the vaqueros who wrote this book."

It is a prescient statement for, if his style has been to a degree polished by his reading, his content directly reflects the *hombres del campo* with whom he rode; it is in the work of Jefe Rojas that this state's vaqueros have found their collective voice.

Down the street, four brown children are kicking a soccer ball and chattering in Spanish. Jefe's hawk eyes—eyes that have watched great condors sweep from the wind to strip the bones of dead sheep, that have seen men now long-dead struggle to pull stranded cattle from Kern River's sucking sands—lock for a moment on those happy youngsters, those *niños* who are growing up in a world remote from the one Jefe once knew on these same ranges, and who may never understand their own intimate heritage in this place. After a moment, the old man smiles and says to me, "It's been an interesting life."

LIBRARY ST. MARY'S COLLEGE

EVERY MAN A SHERIFF [1975]

Yearning for a past that never was, they talk gravely of rising crime rates, of illegal taxes, of the right to bear arms. Their dress is heterogeneous: many tend toward Western attire, pistols slung low on their thighs; other wear official looking uniforms and tote service revolvers; still others wear business suits or blue jeans or work clothes or oddly dated mismatches of Sunday-go-to-meetin' finery. And everyone is armed.

"There is no greater law firm than Smith and Wesson," says Francis Gillings of Stockton, who was recently indicted on tax evasion charges, "especially if it is backed up by a twelve-gauge injunction."

These are the men of Posse Comitatus. The group is, of course, no posse comitatus at all for it has not been organized by local sheriffs but is instead the creation of Mike Beach, a retired laundry equipment salesman from Oregon. Local sheriffs, in fact, seem to be among the vigilante group's principal antagonists.

Beach founded the National Christian Posse Association from his Portland home in 1968, selling charters for $21. He now claims chapters in every state except Hawaii, with nearly 500,000 members (the FBI estimates membership at much closer to 10,000). In any case, Beach has tapped a deep vein of anger and frustration among middle-to-lower-income whites whose economic stability and personal values have been severely assaulted by events of the past ten years.

Combining their anger with the frontier tradition of direct citizen action, a tradition with which they strongly identify, Posse members symbolize a more general mood among those Americans who feel they "foot the bills" and "take it in the ass from everyone." Their most ominous potential is found in the tendency of Posse members, and their growing group of sympathizers, to vent their rage not on actual causes of their distress but on those who are themselves victimized by established power and wealth, by impersonal government, by social prejudices.

Groused a Kern County Posse member: "It's Cesar Chavez and his bunch that've screwed things up for workin' folks around here." The tendency of people near the bottom of the barrel to fight one another rather than their actual foes is again exemplified. In this case, the unenlightened indictments separate many poor whites from any possibility of a broader based movement. So they return to older, often ugly patterns of organization.

In some chapters, the increasingly popular name of White Christian Posse is more appropriate than Posse Comitatus because the former exposes undercurrents of racism, anti-Semitism, and anti-Catholicism that mix with Populism to create a latter-day parody of know-nothingism. However, the Posse's central credo is anti-big government, plus a yearning for simpler, better times. Beach claims: "Our Republic has already gone down the drain. Parasites have come in and destroyed our republican form of government." To date, Posse members have tended not to search for complex answers to complicated problems but to focus instead on visible enemies, scapegoats, the ubiquitous "they." More particularly, the Posse has zeroed in on invasive government and its agents, and on corrupt public officials.

In Petaluma the Posse's leader is Howard G. Sampson, who explains: "Our powers come from above, just as the writers of the Constitution were men inspired by God. Every minister should be a sheriff." Sampson is both a lay preacher and a self-appointed sheriff, his badge purchased for $6.50 from Mike Beach. He was also, until recently, an unlicensed paving contractor.

Sampson believes licensing is illegal because it interferes with free enterprise. Authorities disagreed, however, and the Posse leader found himself in court. Acting as his own attorney (he asked prospective jurors if they believed in God), Sampson promptly subpoenaed eighteen local officials, including the mayor, police chief, sheriff, district attorney and various members of the city council, all of whom he planned to quiz on the Constitution and the Bible. The subpoenas were quashed.

It took fifteen minutes for the jury to find Sampson guilty, which led him to comment: "They weren't independent people who know what freedom means, people who believe in the Constitution."

The Petaluma man's odd mixture of fundamental Christianity, aggrieved self-interest, and selective interpretation of the Constitution symbolizes well the views of Posse members. Said a well-dressed man at a Posse meeting in San Jose: "Did you read about the little Mexican girl that got raped and murdered? Well, the bastard that done it got paroled last month after only four years of a life sentence. Know what he got sent up for the last time? Rape and murder. If I was that little girl's daddy, I'd have to kill me some parole board people, and I ain't shittin'."

The uneven and seemingly unwise administration of justice isn't the only bone stuck in the Posse members' craws. The federal income tax, land-use permits, and licensing are, they claim, unconstitutional. Ecologists are prime targets in logging and ranching country. The only legal law-enforcement officers in the United States are county sheriffs, claims Posse literature. The group has assumed the obligation to rid government, local as well as national, of corrupt public officials, and Mike Beach has suggested public hangings as the best approach.

But Beach does not exercise much control over local chapters, so there is considerable local emphasis on pet issues. In San Joaquin County not long ago, armed Posse members kept organizers of the United Farm Workers from entering a field to recruit. In an ensuing scuffle, a deputy sheriff was nearly hit by an accidental shotgun blast, and the organization reaped a harvest of adverse publicity. Even chapter head Jim McDaniel acknowledged that his people were undertrained in firearms use: "It won't happen again because we're starting a training program."

But more than a training program may be necessary to improve the image of what a Sonoma County deputy called "a bunch of gun-toting amateurs." This is especially true because so many members slip easily—almost automatically—into polar language that sprinkles terms like "Coloreds" and "Mexicans" among generalizations like: "Most of your good ones are ashamed of their race," or "I can't see why any people would want everything given to them."

Members are often walking encyclopedias of unverified "true facts." A Yolo County man explained: "It's not so much your Mexicans I'm against, it's that rotten Chavez. He's put millions and millions of dollars away for his family, but he'll cost workers a raise if they won't join his union." The San Joaquin County chapter has, in fact, been accused of receiving clandestine grower support in exchange for acting as a private police force—an unverified "true fact" which members vigorously deny. In any case, the chapter's members display little familiarity with California's long history of grower-worker problems, and even less knowledge of the economic tension and ethnic caste system such problems reflect.

But the San Joaquin County group is not alone in fighting "un-American" activities. Last year in Wisconsin an agent of the Internal Revenue Service was assaulted and briefly held prisoner while Posse members called him a traitor for enforcing income tax laws, photographed him, and asked him to sign a "public service questionnaire." In Idaho, a group of men surrounded a policeman on his way to testify against a Posse sympathizer, and tried to prevent his testimony. The officer was rescued by a force of deputies.

Speaking to Posse members in Burbank, Terrence Oaks claimed that laws passed by an elected Congress are unconstitutional because Congress itself is ignoring the Constitution. "So we form a posse comitatus. If they do anything about it, they're interfering with common law, and who knows, somebody might shoot them."

Oaks, who was convicted for failure to file a 1971 income tax return and for filing a false withholding exemption form, then exploded: "We've got a criminal government! That's what we've got. I'm not going to live under this. I'll die first. There's going to be some bloodshed. There's only one way they're going to get my gun. They're going to get it out of my cold, dead, clammy fingers!"

Howard Sampson adds: "They [government officials] are taking the rights away from the people and they're passing laws that are unconstitutional. They don't even know the interpretation of the Constitution . . . the rights of the people." The Posse requires no Supreme Court to interpret the Constitution.

The radical Left, that other nebulous force which claims to champion "the people," has figured in the formation of some Posse chapters. According to John Brevard of Grass Valley, "It's things like the bombings that started all this. We want to be ready, not just hiding behind our doors waiting for somebody to come break them down."

Jim McDaniel points out that state and federal laws "require, not suggest," that every male eighteen years old and over "aid and assist in preventing any breach of the peace or the commission of any criminal offense." The actual reason for forming a local posse, he says, "is the rising crime rate, the way courts have tied law-enforcement agencies' hands . . . A law-enforcement agency can't do anything any more without getting in trouble." Publicly, at least, law-enforcement agencies scoff at the Posse.

In its Western branches, the Posse Comitatus has stuck closely to its "pro-Constitution" activities and pretty well avoided the racial and religious nonsense associated with such related groups as the Sons of Liberty, the National States Rights Party, and the Ku Klux Klan; there is at present no evidence linking the Posse formally to other groups, though duplication of membership is not uncommon. Many Posse members are active in American Party politics, and their views adhere closely to those of Governor George Wallace.

Despite claims—sounding perfunctory in most cases— that "lots of doctors and lawyers are members," the visible membership is made up overwhelmingly of blue-collar, working-class people. There are even a few nonwhites, who tend to speak more openly and more strongly against negative trends within their own ethnic groups than do their white colleagues.

White or not, members profess strong beliefs in common law, private property, and traditional Americanism (as they define it). They are incensed by interference with their attempt to structure their lives according to their own values, and they are tired of being scapegoats for a liberal, intellectual elite. "We just wanna live our own lives," explains a Petaluma man.

Above all, like their leftist counterparts, they express intense frustration at the size and impersonality of government, and are angered by the inability of individuals to be heard. Many are contemplating ventures into local politics, for they sense something is deeply wrong and they want to get America "back on the track."

The Posse has so far committed no violence, but members continue to bluster. Observed a Petaluma policeman during a recess in the Sampson trial: "They don't have IQ requirements; they don't test for mental stability, and they *are* armed. And they're pissed. That makes them dangerous." Demands Howard G. Sampson: "If God's for you, then who can be against you?" Then he adds: "There's always been a chosen few."

The sight of grown men desperate enough to pin on fake sheriffs' badges, strap on revolvers, and patrol their areas in official-appearing sedans should lead the rest of us to a serious re-examination of the forces that have produced such vigilante activities. If we don't, our own judgments become as shallow as many of theirs.

WORKIN' MAN'S BLUES [1977]

As we plunge down California's core on Interstate 5, tule fog thickens, absorbs our car in the San Joaquin Valley's dense winter: a gray world in which restaurants, gas stations, and other cars—their lights the eerie eyes of deep sea fishes—loom ghostly, then fade. Through this gloom, near Lost Hills we hear a beacon from Bakersfield, radio station KUZZ/AM sends the familiar nasal tones of Hank Snow to guide us home: "Big eight-wheeler movin' down the track . . ."

West of Shafter on Lerdo Road, back in Kern County, grainy fog still secrets us. Our car's engine suddenly erupts steam and its temperature soars. As I brake, a truck following us also stops and a lean young man wearing a straw cowboy hat joins me examining the engine.

"Havin' trouble?" he asks as Old Faithful forces me away from my auto.

"Yep," I reply.

He offers me a dip from his can of snuff. "Radiator hose looks like," he suggests and, by the time we confirm his diagnosis, another farmer has stopped, and his wife is sharing a thermos of coffee with us. The lean man fetches a roll of tape from his truck and repairs the hose. We all shake hands and once more hit the road.

Forty years ago the tule fog was lonelier, KUZZ wasn't around and Kern County's country music tradition was still being born in the desperate voices of people out of luck in a strange place, their children's bellies swollen with malnutrition. This area's legacy of country music is one of pain endured and hardships overcome because, as local historian Richard Bailey explains, "Country music didn't get started here until the Dust Bowl. The Okies brought it."

Today, no town other than Nashville, and possibly the rockabilly capital, Austin, is as closely identified with country music as Bakersfield. And no place has remained as true to country's traditional sound—*Time* calls it "scruffier, less polished"; we natives call it less pop, more country. Local musicians have their own roots musically as well as personally. Said a sideman at Oildale's now-defunct Cimmaron Club, "See, when they was all listenin' to Eddie Arnold and Elvis, we was still with Lefty [Frizzell] and ol' Hank [Williams]."

There is a sense in which Oildale, not its better-known neighbor, Bakersfield, is the county's locus of country music. Located adjacent oilfields across the Kern River north of the larger city, Oildale is Merle Haggard's hometown and—prejudice revealed—mine. It also houses one of the largest country music complexes on the West Coast, Buck Owens Enterprises. Still unincorporated and now contiguous with Bakersfield, the town is a friendly community inhabited mainly by white working folks, a mini-Southwest where, in my youth, onanistic lads named William and Gerald and Joseph lusted after beautiful girls called Dusty and Tootsie and PeeWee who, in turn, succumbed to the glandular charms of lotharios named Junior and J.D. and Cletus. Many depression migrants settled here and the term "Oildale Okie" became so common that, when the local high school was built in the 1950s, some rakes suggested that its athletic teams be called just that, the Okies. The name actually selected may have presaged the town's present position in the world of country music: the North High Stars.

Whatever it lacked culturally—there was no symphony, no ballet, no opera other than the Grand Ol' on the radio—it was a fine, lively place to grow up. It was not, however, a subtle environment: we all suffered our shares of bloody noses and bruised knuckles, and innocence could be battered by premature sexual encounters, so the community developed a reputation for roughness. Many of us were also exposed to neolithic racial attitudes, polarized social categories, and at least a tad of xenophobia. On the other hand, we grew up in Oildale with a clear vision of life's potentials and problems, and a willingness to face them, and many of us matured to reject the negative aspects of our heritage. Survival is often a matter of trade-offs, and being raised in Oildale provided far more pluses than minuses. Most of all, a work ethic was preached and exemplified—ass up, nose down.

But it is Bakersfield not Oildale whose name and reputation is central in most people's awareness of Kern County and its music. As one California joke has it, the first three words children in Oklahoma learn are "Mommy," "Daddy" and "Bakersfield." The town has been the butt of many barbs; with glitzy Southern California only a hundred miles south, Kern County's seat—another joke—has seemed an easy and frequent target for comics ignorant of the complex if raw ethos of the place. Some years ago, Bakersfield was the subject of a controversial article published in the *Los Angeles Times* Sunday magazine, *West*. Charles Powers rattled local cages with sketches, assertions, and a few insights about the area. One of the latter was that "if there is such a thing as the pure spirit of country music, Bakersfield might genuinely qualify as Number One."

He was right, for Bakersfield and its environs, in spite of continued growth and the influence of two colleges, does retain a frontier quality, a rough edge that is the bane of civic boosters. Some observers suggest that this hardness follows from the harsh weather and the abundance of tough, physical jobs in the area, especially in the agriculture and petroleum industries which dominate the local economy. Bakersfield has been called the northernmost Southwestern community, more Lubbock than San Francisco, with ranchettes, horses, guns, and Western clothing common. Motor vehicles—trail bikes, dune buggies, dragsters, and jeeps—loom large in local lifestyles, and cars in general are taken seriously. You don't have to search very long to see wounded autos in yards or on streets, their engines dangling from A-frames, while one or two shade-tree fix-it men gravely discuss therapeutic options.

In truth, there are many Bakersfields: the established-wealth "elite" who resent and resist the prominence of country music just as they resented and resisted the Okie migration (once the migrants ceased to provide them with economic advantages, anyway); *nouveaux riches* who, in their ostentatious spending frenzies, often seem bent upon outdoing the worst stereotypes of Texans; the substantial population of nonwhites who are struggling as the Okies once struggled to escape the central valley's tradition of agricultural peonage; the large number of white working folks who simply don't care one way or another about local music, but who are proud of the city's improving national image; and business boosters pleased to live in one of America's most prosperous areas. There also exist active theater groups, a symphony association, a historical society and other accoutrements of increasing wealth and encroaching refinement. Predictable in a small town grown large, thin-skinned gentry vociferously resent any interpretation of the area that doesn't jibe with their own, so local artists occasionally feel besieged if their work doesn't conform.

The area also boasts one of the nation's more remarkable athletic traditions. I have seen Frank Gifford and Joey Hernandez, Jeff Seiman and Brent McClanahan, among other future pro's, romp across high school gridirons here. I cheered for Mike Garcia, Johnny Callison and Billy Cowen long before they graced the major league diamonds, and I competed in track meets that featured future Olympic gold medalists such as Leamon King and Rafer Johnson; I watched Davis-Cupper-to-be Dennis Ralston play for Bakersfield High.

Still, football is king and I was raised to believe it unmanly not to play; in retrospect, I have come to recognize that it would have taken more courage not to, certainly more than I had, anyway. A high percentage of local males participated in those years, and few communities of comparable size produced more college and professional players. This has been described in negative terms by critics who see it as the logical product of Bakersfield's "super-macho, overly competitive" atmosphere. In any case, a number of jocks—many of them black—have used athletics to escape the local caste system, or to enter its higher levels. I have come to understand that the best thing about football in Bakersfield for me was that it brought me together with kids from various social and ethnic backgrounds in a setting where who your parents were didn't mean jack. It was brutally egalitarian.

That aforementioned caste system grew in large measure from the interrelated facts that nonwhites have traditionally done stoop labor—migrant farm work—in Kern County, and that wealth and power have historically been concentrated in the hands of a decidedly white few. This produces what might be termed the classic California economic pyramid: a massive base including disproportionately large numbers of brown or yellow or black or red people toiling in desperate conditions so that at the apex a fair-skinned few might enjoy baronial luxury and the accoutrements of power.

The latter reality takes on dimensions unimaginable to most people because the numbers are simply too large: Edward Fitzgerald Beale's nearby Rancho Tejon was the proto-type, with 150,000 acres controlled by 1866: a white owner ramrodding scores of brown-skinned vaqueros. By the 1880s, Henry Miller and Charles Lux had assembled over 700,000 acres in the San Joaquin Valley (of a 3,000,000 acres total); in 1890, the Kern County Land Company was formed with hold-ings of 1,369,576 acres; more recently, an industrious Sicilian immigrant named Joe DiGiorgio built a vast and diverse empire from a farm southeast of Bakersfield, an empire that begins with his 20,000-acre spread near Arvin, and also includes some forty other large farms owned or leased in the state, and also includes a dozen packing sheds, and also includes controlling interest in the Klamath Lumber and Box Company, and also includes three wineries (one of which is the largest in the nation), and also includes the Baltimore Fruit Exchange, and on and on, complete with interlocking director-ships: quite a tidy little "farm," California-style. And everything is dependent upon manual labor of one kind or another, much of it done by nonwhites.

It is not surprising that such large and complex opera-tions as DiGiorgio Farms wield tremendous political clout, both officially and unofficially. What *is* both surprising and revealing is the passion with which many local people decried strikes against DiGiorgio, such as the 1947 holdout and the 1967 boycott, claiming that agriculture was too vulnerable to allow the organization of workers. Conveniently—perhaps blissfully—ignored is the fact that DiGiorgio is a massive corporation, not a quarter-section farm. In fact, DiGiorgio Farms probably employs more lawyers—most of them palefaces, you can bet—than quarter-section spreads do pickers. But there is little reason to single out DiGiorgio; it is but a symbol of corporate agriculture in the San Joaquin Valley. In few places has the American illusion that we are a nation of yeomen farmers been more grotesquely distorted.

As said before, most manual labor on such vast holdings has been performed by nonwhites, and many local Anglos frequently claim that Japanese- and Mexican- and Filipino- and African- and Chinese-Americans are somehow uniquely qualified for such work. As a result, nonwhites for a long time provided a convenient bottom for the local class structure. They also provided a mobile, cheap labor force that has, like sunshine or water, been taken for granted by growers, and seasonal unemployment has been accepted gracefully hereabouts by those who reap the benefits of such conditions, if not by those who actually reap the crops. Thus, when Cesar Chavez, Larry Itliong, Dolores Huerta, and company managed to organize farm labor in nearby Delano, it was clear to folks who evidenced no particular understanding of what the word meant that a "communist" plot was afoot.

An earlier farm labor problem occurred in the late 1930s when Okies—whose presence slowed unionization of field labor, by the way—muddled comfortable assumptions by doing what some called "nigger work." Since they had the audacity to be white, the Okies posed a particular threat to the caste system—they might, after all, be confused with "good" whites; moreover, they suffered some of the same blatant discrimination that had previously been reserved for nonwhites. A sign at a Bakersfield movie theater in the 1930s said it all: "Niggers and Okies upstairs."

LIBRARY ST. MARY'S COLLEGE

The long-term outcome of such experiences remains in question, but certainly many lyrics by Merle Haggard reflect an awareness of mutual suffering that is unequalled in country music. One black country singer who is popular in California, and who performs in the tradition of Kern County favorite Lefty Frizzell, is Stoney Edwards; he opens his show with "Poor Folks Stick Together." But the image of a coalition of poor folks sticking together is, to say the least, idealized. During the halcyon days of the United Farm Workers, college students from the Bay Area and Southern California flocked in convinced that soon students and what they called—incanted, really, with neo-religious zeal—"workers" would unite. Whatever else students may have accomplished, such a unification eluded them; they are now back in Westwood or Berkeley or Cambridge and their idealized "workers" are still sweating in Kern County. What is convenient to ignore is that poor folks too often blame one another for their poverty, while the Kern County Land Company and its progeny blissfully pocket profits. A visible scapegoat seems preferable to a vast and clever opponent and, near the bottom of the barrel, punches and accusations tend to be thrown in a swirl of frustration that resembles a two-headed man fighting himself.

Another predictable consequence of Bakersfield's economic conditions is that it is one of the state's conservative enclaves, or so voting records indicate, although some locals are convinced that too many liberals have moved in of late. Nonetheless, political arguments here—especially those heard on local radio—occasionally sound like parodies to outsiders. Listening to talk shows indicates that not only is the world sunk in sin but that Jews have finalized their plans to make "true Christian Americans" their pawns. The "Pope of Rome" fools few in Kern County, and FDR's "sellout" to Stalin did not pass unnoticed. Then there's the white harem that was kept by Martin Luther King, Jr., Cesar Chavez's hidden millions, the plot behind fluoridation, and "our martyred president," decidedly *not* Kennedy. One woman talked at great length about zoning: "The first thing communists do is take over private property," she pointed out, "and that's just what's happenin' here."

Bakersfield is not scenic, although it has pretty neighborhoods. It spreads protoplasmally beyond its official limits in all directions today, threatening to engulf Arvin and Shafter as it has Oildale. The town slopes from Kern River bluffs on its northeast side, hard against a major oilfield, onto the flats where once that Sierran stream flooded annually, creating swamps and shallow lakes that harbored tropical diseases such as malaria and encephalitis. To the east, south and west lie verdant, cultivated fields, desert metamorphosed by irrigation. The city itself squats with earthquake-resistant buildings near the southern extreme of California's Great Central Valley, often in a puddle of smog. On clear winter days, though, with snow-capped peaks visible on three sides, it possesses a sudden grandeur.

The frequently oppressive air pollution, both highly visible and potentially dangerous, especially during the scorching summers, symbolizes local laissez-faire attitudes toward development and commerce. The business of Kern County remains business. Recently, an oil executive told a service club that air quality controls would "have a devastating effect" on the economy of Kern County. He did not mention the effect of pollution on the health of a county where suspicious clusters of diseases have been reported.

Many Kern residents have long resisted government incursions into their lives, pointing to the region's prosperity as evidence for the efficacy of their work-oriented, anti-government-handout philosophy. While such attitudes are inconsistent—big agriculture deserves subsidies, big petroleum merits oil depletion allowances, but little people will be corrupted by government aid, or so the argument goes—it is nonetheless revered with devotion worthy of a saint's bones. Kern County ranks first nationally in petroleum production, second in agriculture, and those two subsidized industries boast enormous influence locally.

Also profoundly influential are Bakersfield's brahmans, the old families, purveyors of established wealth and prejudice. Some of them were involved in Kern County's Committee of Sixty, which became the anti-Okie California Citizens Association in 1939. The *Bakersfield Californian* has for years been the sole influential newspaper in the region, and it is a good one. Locally owned, it has predictably reflected the values of established wealth in its coverage of controversial subjects: during the 1930s, for example, it became anti-migrant after big agriculture decided the Okies were more trouble than they were worth; when they were providing cheap labor and no social upheaval, growers and newspapers alike found the migrants tolerable.

Milton "Spartacus" Miller, a local politician, has not been a favorite of brahmans. Owner of a large downtown hotel, Miller retaliated to a campaign of harassment—fire laws, for example, were to force him to close whole floors of his building—by festooning his building with huge signs visible throughout downtown Bakersfield ("FALSITY RULES THIS TOWN"), by bombarding local newspapers with letters, by publicly fighting rulings intended to hamstring him, and by winning a seat on the Kern County board of supervisors, thus demonstrating a general dissatisfaction with old politics. His appeal was to those who themselves felt gouged by taxes and manipulated by Our Gang politicians. "This really isn't a bad town," Miller told Charles Powers. "But in order to grow, it's got to have about fifteen funerals."

With or without funerals, the local ruling order is churning. Selected members of the newly rich are inducted into it, a survey of boards of directors reveals, yet the power base remains narrowly and tightly controlled. Utilizing local media, it is possible to play the aspirations and anxieties of economically strapped people against one another, as the widespread opposition to welfare for the poor illustrates: "They just want our hard-earned tax dollars."

They, in fact, is a favorite word when discussing social issues; it means "the others," "those who would take what we've got"; it means "the dark ones." Moreover, its incantation evokes metaphysical fear in people emerging from economically deprived backgrounds, people who are desperate not to lose what they've so recently gained. That this is a false "we/they" dichotomy is generally only recognized by those in a position to benefit from others not recognizing it, so it is a truth rarely addressed. Attacks on excessive concentrations of power or bloated business are apt to be skillfully deflected as a threat to working people of the area: "*They* will take your jobs." "*They* will take your daughters." "*They* will take your country."

Then there is the assertion of some Auslanders that Kern County is an enclave of Ku Klux Klan types. In the 1960s, the region was reputed to harbor the largest White Citizen's Council outside the Deep South—a claim that was never proven, by the way—and a while back Negro leaders in Bakersfield charged police brutality after a fight at a college dance. That any blacks *attended* a dance at Bakersfield College, however, evidences social growth because when I was a student there in the 1950s, "coloreds," as they are still frequently called, attended classes and participated on teams, but only rarely showed up for social functions. They had their own social lives, or so we assumed.

Interestingly enough, formal affairs were more apt to be somewhat integrated then—the prom, for example—while after-game hops tended to be segregated. The constraints of civilization always loomed larger in tuxedos, and the gulp-a-beer-and-take-a-swing losers generally avoided formal dances. I also recall a few class and student body officers who were Afro-Americans, sharp folks like Jackie Wallace, James Shaw and Naaman Brown, and some quite tentative social contacts, so I guess we managed to sow a few seeds during the mid-fifties, but in general we did not do much—certainly not enough—to challenge racial assumptions.

I must admit that we not only didn't see blacks at post-game dances or parties but that we also didn't note their absence. We would have unquestionably taken notice had blacks chosen to attend. The same generalization, slightly altered of course, can be applied to Chicanos and Asian-Americans, although it was permissible, just barely so, to date them if they were well assimilated; as one Oildale chum observed when I was dating a lovely Chicana, "There's Mexicans and then there's Mexicans." In any case, while some whites would have welcomed sudden social integration even then, the majority clearly would not have. "They want to go too fast," was a frequent observation in those days.

Still, with blacks attending sock hops at BC and racial restrictions for various jobs being dropped—most dramatically, the integration of oil field work—conditions seem somewhat better, although de facto segregration in local schools is being investigated by the Department of Health, Education, and Welfare, leading many locals to urge the school board to tell the Feds to shove their money. The major reason for such segregation is that many blacks and Chicanos cluster in their own districts, largely due to poverty but also because whites tend to depart when nonwhites move into a middle-class neighborhood; paradoxically, those same whites then assert that *they*—the coloreds—move in and take over, ignoring the fact that *they* can't buy houses that are not for sale. Increasingly, though by no means commonly, whites and nonwhites are living side by side, something unheard of a generation ago when "They're happier with their own" could justify discrimination both overt and covert. However slowly, change continues.

What does country music have to say about such developments? Merle Haggard leads the way, having acknowledged early in his career the debt his music owes to the blues and the black people who created that wondrous music. In songs such as "White Man Singing the Blues," he has made the relationship explicit, and he has alluded to the fact that poor whites and poor blacks have a great deal in common. He has also sung about one consequence of shared poverty, interracial love, in "Irma Jackson," breaking a long-standing code of silence on such subjects.

Country has been poor folks' music mainly because the region that spawned it, the American South, has traditionally endured considerable poverty. Within the region, however, the music has boasted fans from all classes and the same is true in Kern County, where many second-generation Okies have moved well up the socio-economic ladder. As a result, such fabled nightclubs as the Blackboard, the Lucky Spot, and

Tex's Barrel House—all now *hors de combat*—over the years attracted an increasingly affluent, increasingly diverse clientele.

In the 1950s, the Blackboard, featuring Terry Preston (aka Ferlin Husky), Jean Sheppard, Tommy Collins, Herb Henson, Jimmy Thomason, Fuzzy Owen, Lewis Talley, Buck Owens, among others, attracted large crowds every weekend; it was also reputed to have hosted more fights than Madison Square Garden. Whether fighting or dancing, the mood was set by what locals called "Okie music," for Bakersfield was the hub of the great migration into California in the thirties. The area's abundance of jobs in agriculture and petroleum originally attracted migrants to Kern County; between 1935 and 1940, the county's population increased by a whopping 52,554 souls (63.3 percent). In Bakersfield and Oildale, plus such nearby communities as Arvin, Lamont, Pumpkin Center, Weedpatch, McFarland, Wasco, Shafter and Delano, Okies settled, bringing their folklore, their values, and their speech as well as their music. The so-called Okies were not all from Oklahoma, of course, and not all were Dust Bowl refugees. Says radio personality "Okie Paul" Westmoreland, "To me the Okies are anyone who picked that cotton for 50¢ a hundred pounds, or picked potatoes for 15¢ an hour." If today the children of those migrants are Californians, the Golden State itself has been altered by the migration in a number of subtle, significant, not-always-acknowledged ways.

For instance, Okies resisted welfare during the old days; only in February when there was almost no field labor available did rural welfare rolls grow significantly. Their contemporary disdain for the dole is also consistent. Recalls Westmoreland: "We've always known how to work. God a'mighty did we work. Had to, or starve." They toiled—at first, anyway—at jobs menial and tough. Okies were reputed to give an employer an honest jump for his money. Work, to a generation that survived the depression, took on nearly mystical qualities: you could tell a guy's character by how he worked. The question of *if* he worked need not be raised. A Shell Oil foreman in Oildale during the early sixties, upset by civil rights activities, told me: "Hell, those coloreds don't want equality, they want priority. If

they just *worked* they'd be okay." Such simplistic, sincere pro-
nouncements were frequently heard in my all-white hometown
during those years.

The work ethic endures in the Bakersfield area. In one of
his finest songs, "Workin' Man's Blues," Haggard captures these
elements: "I'll be out workin'/ long as these two hands/ are fit
to use." A man labors to support his family, a woman toils to
hold it together, and everyone who amounts to anything
works. Like many who grew up in Kern County, I boast college
degrees and a comfortable life today in no small measure
because my father labored for some forty years in the region's
oil fields and my mother held our family together. One generation sacrifices so that the next may prosper, and hereabouts
the system seems to suffice; it has far more advocates than
critics.

Probably the most interesting effect of the depression
migration has been to create a traditionalist buffer that resists
California's apparently promiscuous trendiness: the Great
Central Valley, where many Southwesterners settled, is culturally a vast distance from the hot tub and white wine and
swishy tan image of the state. Hard work, beer, church and
family loom larger than "doing lunch" and "relationships";
physical confrontations and traditional sexual roles are common, thus encounters, not encounter groups, have been the
rule; the Protestant Ethic hovers always near the surface here.
And there is a sense of a shared past.

When I was a kid, on long summer evenings in the 1940s,
fiddle and guitar music drifted from fenceless yards in Oildale
as working men—their forearms burned brown as jerky, their
hands thick and hard—gathered to sing about old days and
other places. They sat on porch steps or in wooden kitchen
chairs with wives and children around them, joining them to
sing about Pretty Boy Floyd or how faith in Jesus would always
see them through. We kids were full of envy for those few of our
number who could play the mouth harp or guitar and were
admitted to the musician's circle. There was a girl in our
neighborhood who sang with a high clear voice that quieted all

others, and neighbors would leave their houses to hear her. Womenfolk—some wearing sun bonnets—stood with arms folded, humming along; men, their backs crossed by galluses, thrust hands into jean pockets and nodded. Long after dark, our mothers would call us in and, especially if someone had brought a jar of liquor or a bag of beer, the music trilled on and on.

In such fashion, country music infiltrated Kern County's culture so that by the 1960s it was acknowledged, even by those who had developed no taste for it, to be a major local attribute. Lately, a pop version of country has infiltrated the mainstream, in part because of a syrupy Americanism that has been found to generate easy sales; this music arose from the old Confederacy, leading an Oildale pal—his family migrants from Tennessee—to suggest, "Hey, us Rebs are gonna win with guitars what we couldn't with guns."

As was true of the South, there was considerable action at big dance halls hereabouts as well as honky tonks years ago, because the former allowed whole families to enjoy the music together at places like the Beardsley Ballroom, the Barn, and Rainbow Gardens where sons and daughters, grandmas and grandpas, did occasionally dip and swirl to the twang of what we called "High-wine" (Hawaiian) steel guitars. Other family dances were held on open-air cement pads in the Bakersfield area at places like Kern County Park or the Kern River Golf Course or at "camps" owned by various oil companies.

After picnics or barbecues, drinks flowing freely—some men sipping from bottles in paper bags, even Four Roses tasting like nectar—a local band would begin playing, slightly out of rhythm, slightly out of tune at first, but sounding better as the evening wore on, or so it seemed, those paper bags performing their magic. At other times, records would be played, low fidelity and loud, and mothers would dance with adolescent sons, a little startled yet proud that these young stallions were theirs, while fathers eyed boys eyeing daughters. The music like the people was country.

So there was a solid, if little known, country music tradition in Kern County long before its recent prominence, and a central figure who played at those ballrooms and honky tonks and county parks, and who contributed mightily to what makes local music important, was Bill Woods, an Okie who drifted into Bakersfield in the 1930s. Acknowledges Betty Azevedo, Merle Haggard's long-time secretary, "Bill Woods was the granddaddy. You have to give him credit for all of it, because he was here when nobody else was around." Woods formed a band—the Orange Blossom Playboys—that entertained around town, most notably at the Blackboard. I remember him from those days as a stocky man whose eyes sometimes closed to creases when he sang in a moaning baritone, and whose hair occasionally fell onto his forehead. His music could hardly have been called progressive—Azevedo characterizes it as "pure old hillbilly"—and fittingly so, since it presaged the traditional country sound for which the area is now famous. Woods opened his bandstand to newcomers, providing a considerable boost up the ladder for many. Says Haggard, who wrote and recorded a song about Woods, "In Bakersfield, that same helpin' hand just kept reachin' out time after time."

Country music began its climb to big business in Kern County in the 1950s when popular local television shows warred for audiences. Fiddler Jimmy Thomason and piano-plunking Cousin Herb Henson were the early favorites. By the mid-fifties, Cousin Herb's show dominated, with Jelly Sanders, Bonnie Owens, and Fuzzy Owen, the Farmer Boys from Farmersville, and a seemingly endless parade of local kids.

Henson seems to be something of a forgotten man today, but my family and a great many others never missed his hokey, entertaining afternoon show that always included a *hymn* (pronounced with two syllables) and frequently sent greetings to "our shut-in *friends*" (also two syllables). The chubby Cousin seemed to be another neighbor, and his convivial approach rescued country music from its rough, honky-tonk image locally, thus widening its audience considerably.

Another channel soon countered with Billy Mize fronting a group that featured Buck Owens. Those shows seemed to be a ready route to fame and I remember my envy when a classmate appeared on *both* programs in a single month. She's a housewife in Bakersfield today, but not without memories. In any case, all three programs were uneven and could be implausibly corny, but all three presented wholesome images of country musicians—occasionally featuring the families of performers—and all three also highlighted some entertainers who would one day become major figures in country music. I remember especially Ferlin Husky, then known as Terry Preston, with a curl falling down his forehead, crooning in a syrupy baritone while Cousin Herb grinned in the background. I don't know if I more envied the curl or the voice.

It was truly the emergence of Buck Owens as a superstar that riveted national attention on Bakersfield as a country music citadel. In Nashville, some folks still call this town "Buckersfield," and not without reason, for few more astute businessmen have ever worn overalls and picked guitar. Alvis Edgar Owens, Jr., who grew up in Sherman, Texas, and Mesa, Arizona, is a self-taught musician who had been working as an entertainer since he appeared on a Mesa radio show at the age of sixteen. In 1951, he moved to Bakersfield where he played guitar and sang at the Blackboard, and earned extra cash as a studio musician in Hollywood. His flat, appealing features and short blond hair were familiar to television viewers during the 1950s, as were many of the songs he wrote. Then as now, his music featured a strong beat, with more than a hint of both Western swing and rock'n'roll. He explains, "I was influenced by all the greats, but I never played . . . those types of affairs where people sit down. From Arizona to Bakersfield, I played dances . . . and those people want rhythm. They want to dance." In 1960 he cut "Under Your Spell Again" for Capitol, and his career as a recording artist took off. He has seldom looked back.

He is popular with his Kern County neighbors because, despite his reputation as a tough employer and a perfectionist, he has been public spirited in the best sense of the term, sponsoring an annual celebrity golf tournament with proceeds going to the American Cancer Society. He has also worked mightily to help build a new oncology center at Bakersfield Memorial Hospital. He continues living just north of town on Poso Creek, and he moves easily with the city's elite. A few years ago, Buck Owens Day was officially proclaimed in Bakersfield.

If Buck remains the head of country music in Kern County, then Merle Haggard is its heart. The son of Okies who migrated to California in 1934, Merle was born in Bakersfield in April of 1937, a month after I was. He grew up just three blocks west of me in Oildale, within hailing distance of where Buck Owens Enterprises now stands across from Standard School, which Merle and I attended. Unfortunately, that nearly exhausts my knowledge of Merle's childhood because, although we were classmates, we were not close friends, merely acquaintances. He suffered a terrible loss when he was nine: the death of his beloved father. "Merle's daddy died," kids whispered; I heard it, but only recently have I begun to comprehend what it meant.

But I do remember—or have I invented it?—that he grew hard to get along with about then. He and I had a couple of schoolyard scraps and I began to hear that he was hanging out with "bad" kids. Shortly thereafter, our class was "tracked" into five groups and I recall that the youngster who would develop into one of the most inventive minds in country music was placed near the bottom—so much for intelligence testing. About that time, too, Merle and Billy Thorp, who lived down the block, became sudden celebrities among neighborhood kids because they hopped a freight train and rode to Fresno. I envied them for years.

A while later, I heard stories at Bunky's Drive-In or at the River Theater, Oildale's two teenage gathering places, about Merle's exploits as a fighter or lover or adventurer, but by then my folks had sent me to the Catholic high school in Bakersfield, and I seldom communicated with him except for an occasional nod—sometimes belligerent, sometimes friendly, in the manner of adolescent males—when we passed on El Tejon Avenue.

In any case, the kid I knew and the man I don't are the same in some essential ways. Merle lets his background show in songs like "Momma Tried," which concludes, "That leaves only me to blame 'cause momma tried," as indeed Mrs. Haggard did, and if the results in the short run were disturbing, perhaps the long run has made them acceptable. Deepened by such things as spending seven of his first twenty-one years behind bars, Merle achieves an honesty and power in his songs rare in country's history. The man *is* his music, and Hag remains without question the most important oral poet produced by California Okies because many of his songs seem to draw on some deep resource of communal experience that approaches the archetypal.

Haggard had been raised in a musical family and his friends had known he could sing way back in the Bunky's Drive-In days. His father, James, had led a small band in Oklahoma before moving west, and he was one of the neighborhood musicians who made those Oildale evenings more pleasant. The combination of innate ability, family tradition, and the popularity of country music in Kern County during his childhood provided Merle with a strong foundation when his own singing and composing career blossomed.

He is musically a throwback who does not need electronically enhanced presentations, whose sensitive baritone voice is better when not overaccompanied, and whose songs illustrate social awareness and humor as well as suffering and pragmatism. There is irony in the prominence given a number such as "Okie from Muskogee" for it tapped deep wells of resentment and confusion among people who had themselves long been the subjects of jokes and simplistic lyrics in songs by folk and rock entertainers.

Ironically, "Okie" started as a humorous and obviously satiric song—"We don't smoke marijuana in Muskogee/ We don't take our trips on LSD." They may not smoke marijuana in Muskogee, but you can bet that a few joints have been toked in Haggard's tour bus. Merle was shocked by the outburst that followed the song's release: "Boy," he told Paul Hemphill, "I didn't realize how strong some people felt about those things."

Ironically, Haggard is among the most open minded in a business noted for sloganistic conservatism, as even *Rolling Stone* has admitted. While he had occasionally indulged in the same simplistic psuedo-patriotism that characterizes the work of lesser artists, unlike them he had also written with power of disenfranchisement and disenchantment in the world's richest nation.

He has not developed his perceptions abstractly. In his hometown, he can find an abundance of folks who with good reason believe that America works; the mother of a mutual friend observed when he was awarded his degree in electrical engineering, "Who'd a thought . . ." She had struggled into California as a marginally educated young woman during the depression and had endured considerable poverty. She had also lived to see all three of her children—very much Californians—graduate from college, one with a Ph.D. A uniquely American sociological phenomenon frequently emerges in such conditions: an educationally bifurcated family—smart, but poorly educated, sometimes poverty-stricken older generation; highly motivated, thus highly educated younger generation. While loaded subjects such as politics and religion are often left undiscussed in such families, real rancor is rare because children understand full well that they are the product of opportunities denied their parents yet made possible by them; together, they have *lived* the emergence from poverty. Bonds of love tend to transcend potential problems, although complete understanding is rarely achieved.

Unfortunately, have-nots don't always beget haves, so Merle refuses to ignore in his lyrics the tragic gap between rich and poor that also characterizes the Bakersfield area—that economic pyramid alluded to earlier—as illustrated by such songs as "If We Make It Till December" and "Hungry Eyes." A sort of applied pragmatism informs his lyrics; as a result, his greatest strength is his ability to capture the concerns of common people, their symbols and meanings, with directness and dignity: at his best he reaches our heads via our guts no matter what the subject of his song:

And I won't have to wonder who she's had,
No, it's not love,
But it's not bad . . .

Merle has PBS tattooed on his wrist, a reminder of a sojourn in Preston Boys' School, a state reformatory sometimes referred to as prep school for San Quentin—where he later matriculated—and carries his experiences with him as he does that one, not as baggage, but as material, his pleasure and pain becoming ours when he writes about them.

One day a few summers back a man followed me out of an Oildale grocery store, then called my name in the parking lot. He was Peanut Renfrow, a classmate at Standard School whom I hadn't seen for at least twenty years. We leaned on my car—me chewing, him smoking—and talked about old times and old friends. It turned out that Peanut owned the store and a good deal more. Our conversation turned to Merle, and Peanut said, "He had some tough times, but he always stayed a good guy. You know what he does now, him living way on the other side of town by Kern Canyon? He still drives out to Oildale to buy his groceries from me." He grinned and shook his head. I knew what he meant.

He was talking about exactly the quality that makes the best country music from the Bakersfield area special. Merle and Peanut are moving up and they're taking their music with them, but they haven't forgotten who they are or where they've come from. As a result, country music from Kern County is less sullied by market surveys, more sullied by how actual human beings think and feel. And that is where all great art must begin, with the actual experiences of people.

About the Author

GERALD HASLAM is a fourth-generation Californian—a paternal great-grandfather having migrated west from upstate New York after the Civil War, while a maternal great-grandmother traveled north from Mexico at about the same time. He is a native of Oildale, a small town near Bakersfield at the southern end of the Great Central Valley.

Known primarily as a writer of short fiction, he has published four collections of stories to date: *Okies* (1973), *The Wages of Sin* (1980), *Hawk Flights: Visions of the West* (1983), and *Snapshots: Glimpses of the Other California* (1985). Number five, *The Man Who Cultivated Fire: California Stories*, is scheduled for release later this year by Capra Press. He has also published one novel, *Masks* (1976), and edited a series of literary anthologies: *Forgotten Pages of American Literature* (1970), *Western Writing* (1974), and *California Heartland* (with James D. Houston, 1978), and *A Literary History of the American West* (with Thomas J. Lyon, et al., 1987).

Haslam has also been an essayist of note, with social and literary pieces appearing in some seventy-five journals and anthologies. Observed Gerald Locklin in his study of Haslam in the Western Writers Series (Number 77, Boise State University, 1987), "His stories have, in any case, established him as a leading Western fictionalist of his generation, and his critical, scholarly, and general articles have secured his place as a foremost contemporary commentator on 'the Other California'—the state's rural and small-town areas, especially the Great Central Valley."

Like his boyhood chum Merle Haggard, Haslam has never forgotten who he is or where he comes from, so perhaps more than any other writer, his stories and essays have explored the California ignored by the state's stereotype. His places are as real as dirt clods and searing sun, his people as vital as the Chinese or Portuguese or black migrants who helped build the actual California. As Penelope Reedy suggests, Haslam's writing provides "insights into the diverse lives of people off the main thoroughfares of this myth-laden state."

Although his writing reveals the profound influence of packing sheds and cotton fields and oil rigs, Haslam was formally educated at Bakersfield College, San Francisco State University, Washington State University, and the Union for Experimenting Colleges and Universities, from which he was awarded a Ph.D. in 1980. The father of five children, he and his wife, Jan, live in Northern California where he is Professor of English at Sonoma State University.

LIBRARY ST. MARY'S COLLEGE